ARMOUR WHEREIN HE T

by

Mary Webb

Armour Wherein He Trusted

Being the Say of Lord Gilbert of Polrebec, Afterward the Holy and Pious Abbot of Strata Florida

IN the forest are many voices, and no man riding under the leaves hears the same voice as his companion. For they are diverse as the steep winding paths up into Heaven-Town, to which no man can come by any other way than that his own torch shows him, though the good burgesses leaning over the battlements, picking their teeth, should shout a plain direction to him.

For though one says, 'Come thou through the brake fern, there to the left,' and another says 'No, yonder by the great yew-tree!' and a third crieth that he must go through the deep heather, yet he knows that his one only way is by the Christ-thorn gleaming above the chasm.

So in the forest a man must hear with his own ears the carol that is for him, and one will hear a very sad song, with pine-trees in it, rasping needle on needle and cone on cone, and another will hear flutes and dulcimers afar, as you hear on the white roads of holy Italy. Nor will a man well stricken in years hear the same music as a lad.

So I, riding alone in the oak woods, wending towards Powis (which as all men know is in the Marches of Wales, a savage country in part, but quieter in Sciropshire and ruled and misruled by the Lords Marchers), a young knight in my hey-day, being then one score and three years, lusty, care-free and love-free, heard in the springing April forest on every side the voices of faeries, lively and mocking and beguiling. Not near, nor very far, but where the trees drew together, even where the mist began, they were, hovering in a cloud like midges on a summer day.

Though my eyes were keen enough, I might peer and peer, but see nought of them, not so much as a wing-tip or a gleam of flaxen hair. But in the great stillness of the day I could hear them, mourning like doves, laughing like woodpeckers, shivering into a scatter of sweet notes like painted glass in fragments, belling like frogs in the marishes.

The scurrels ran in the sparse-leaved tree-tops, red as raddle, mazed with spring. I laughed out, and the noise of it startled a herd of wild ponies feeding in the silent forest, so that they took fright, and drove across our way, and my good stallion, heady with grass, gave a grunt and was after them. So it chanced I came to Powis by a roundabout way, through a vasty grove of oaks that were hung and garlanded as for a festival with yellowing mistletoe. All was so still—still as a dewpond. The great oaken boughs were a little leafy with young red leaves, and they spread and towered in the quiet, minding them of the centuries, aye, minding them of the hour that was so still, a thousand years gone and more, when the midnight grew sudden-sweet and small flowers were where had been none, and bells spoke in the meady, golden air, and the thin echo of voices came upon the land—

'Pax vobiscum! Christus natus est.'

The oaks called it to mind. Though storms ravened, they seemed ever at their orisons, and never did I come there but a stillness fell upon me. My good horse stopped, snuffing the air, staring, sweating, then hung his head, hearing, as I know well, beneath the sea-voices of the high boughs—

'Christus natus est.'

I left him standing there and went softly on, over the stag-moss. All was so holy, I was glad I was dressed in my best green coat and my hat with a grey goose feather, for it was as if I went to the Easter Supper.

After a while, I saw that in the midst of the oak grove was a thicket of Christ-thorn, bravely budded. So I went into the thicket, thinking I might find an altar there. But there was no altar, only a small bower woven of wattles and decked out with bunches of early flowers—marigolds and the flowers of young hyacinthus, and the day's eye. Small, nimble birds made claw-marks in the soft earth about it, and the merles sang as if none but faeries ever came there.

'It is a witchen-house,' I said. 'I shall be put in a spell.' And even as I spoke, one looked from the small window of the bower, and behold! it was my love. I knew it was my love, though I had never seen her afore, and I was bewildered, standing like an oaf, looking upon her under the leaves. I mused on her long, struck, as the heron is when he sees his mate imaged in the water. She seemed not troubled at all, to have a great fellow standing there, and by this I was sure she was a faery, since they know not fear.

'Alas!' I said, 'I am a man doomed, for I love a faery, an Ill Person.'

Then on a sudden she laughed, high and brisk, yet with a sound of rain going in the trees. And she rose up and came stooping from the low door, and stooping looked up at me from under her forehead with its clumps of pleated golden hair on this side and on that side. So looking up while yet her chin nestled against the sheepskin of her coat, her face, that was pointed like one of the Small People's faces, seemed even more pointed, like some forest creature—a scurrel, say, or a fox-babe or a vole. Then she straightened and stood like a wand, solemn, as one offended. And she said—

'Sir, I am no Ill Person. I am my Lady Powis's new waiting-woman out of Wales, where are no tall tousle-haired gentlemen that stare upon a maid in her bower.'

3

And turning aside, she seemed to be looking very carefully at the small clouds that came over the tree-tops each after other, like ptarmigan in winter. So I fell into a muse also, for it seemed that there was no other thing any lady could do so fitly as to watch the white ptarmigan in the meadows of God. And I mind this was ever her manner—to make all she did seem the only thing that could be done. For if she leaned over the battlements, or stirred simples over the hearth fire, or sewed her tapestry, it seemed to all that she could do none other thing. And if she sate at the banquet, she seemed in a shrine, as if a great boss of white roses was her chair-back. Never did I see any woman so favouring Our Lady. So a man coming on a dark night to a church with a bright painted window such as they have in Rome, seeing the Mother of God done in lovely blues and raddles, would say 'Ah me! when was the Flower of the West in holy Italy?' For that was her name—leastways among men. Women had other names for her. But men called her ever 'Flower of the West,' and indeed she was at that time, and to me at all times, the fairest woman from Chester to the Southern Sea. Men would fight for a look and die for a smile. But that was after. On this day she was yet a very simple maid, and abashed.

So when we had stood a little while thus, I said—

'If you are no Ill Person, look on me, not on the ptarmigan of heaven. They are not fain of you.'

'Be you, sir?' she said.

And when I answered nothing, for the hoost that love gave, she came nigher and held out her little arms, long like an angel's, and asked again—

'Be you?'

But I said nothing, for she ever put a silence on me, so that I felt my heart brasting with a mort of words—yet not one would come. Words were never good serfs to me. They would stand at gaze, like wild ponies on the mountains, and just when I thought I had tamed one, away it would go with a toss of its mane and leave me all wildered. So my mother would call me the Silent Man and said I was like him that was wiled away by a light in the northern sky, and came where enchanted colours ruled the dark, and was so mazed that he fell into a dream and stood there, freezing, winter by winter, till he was all one great icicle. Misliking the thought of this, I fought with my words, but never till this latter end and sunset of my days have they come at call. Now God sends them, that I may tell in proper fashion all the changes and chances He led me through. Even the long words now, and the Latin words, are biddable. Yet I think the best words tell not much of Him, nor of us, nor of the green, sappy pine forests and nesses of ermine-breasted birds, and rufous bitches suckling their young in dim places, and God speaking in the thunder, moving a mountain yonder, a pyatt here, calling on the seas.

4

And I think my good father was in agreement with me in this, for when mother chid me for my quietness, he would say 'What ails the lad? Would you have him glib as a Norman?' And mother sighed, for she was of Norman blood, and came over with the ladies of King William (may God rest him) and was wed with my father a little while after. For when he saw her he was filled with a fury to have her, as his manner was all through life. Knowing well what liked him, he would have it, whether it was a collop or a lady. He would set his heart on one piece of roast, and woe to the servant who brought any other. And he would suddenly cry out for a manchet or a bowl of mead, and if it tarried he would knock the lad down and be done with him. I speak this, not to bring my father into your ill graces, who read this say of mine, but because it is truth, and I must speak truth or nothing. Especially must I say this because in a measure I inherited this suddenness from my father, so that delay always fretted me, and a nay-word drove me mad. This was a great temptation to me, and gave Satan much power, so if it had not been for my Friend, even the Lord Christus, being ever with me even in my curst youth, I should maybe have killed a man every day. But he was continually near—in the tourney and in the house, in the hour when I took Nesta (that was my love's name) to be my wife, and in the hour when I met my enemy upon the battlements. Times, I could feel as it were a touch on my shoulder. Times, He would look upon me as He did upon Peter (God rest him) and I would fall upon my knees and weep. But other times, though He beguiled me with all the winning kindness of His heart, I would not hearken. So children break their maumets of clay and trample on their crusts of bread in evil rage, and sob a long while after, to think that now they have no crust and no maumet. So we, when we kill and hate and are given to lust and know not rightly what is ours and what is another's, when we smite our beloveds and fling away the Bread of Heaven, must sob a long while in the evening. And He will say 'Hush now, sleep awhile and forget that you hunger. I give you not back the bread you threw to the wolf-dogs, nor the maumet you broke. I take not the weal from your love's face nor bid the varlet you killed to arise and walk. I cannot because I will not, seeing I give you leave to walk with me knowing good and evil and taking your own choice. Another time, let you hearken to me, brother.' O, His kindness cut me to the heart! I would vow to lead the life of the holiest monk, with no devil in it, nor even a foul word. And then I would see a fair face or fall into a brawl or swill mead like a hog, and all the repenting to do over again.

And when your heart and your longings are like a great river flowing strongly, and all dammed up because you have no words, there must come a day when all is carried away, even the banks.

So now, as I looked upon my love's face like alabaster, or rather like the soft petal of some thick fragrant flower, as if she said, 'I am white, but I am also warm,' the thick blood was pounding like galloping horses in my ears, that were hot and burning as my face was and my hands that twitched and sweated. I could see under the sheepskin her robe of silk, that did not hide her as the smocks of the sewing-women and my mother's heavy homespun woollens hid them, but betrayed her to me, seeming to melt away and leave her at my mercy with her small, smooth shoulders sloping like a gracious hillside, and her two breasts round as bowls under the silk, and her lissom body, small as some slim bird until it came to the thigh, and there sweetly rounded. I pray God He will pardon all such talk, for I must tell it, or none can know how things came to pass nor why I was as I was, nor what temptation Satan kept for Nesta. For, though he tempts all women, he has snares for such as Helen of Troy Town which he will not waste on many. And Nesta was of Helen's breed. I suppose she drave more men to madness and damnation than any woman in our country this many a year. Yet not Nesta only, but the wild earth of which she was made, red rock and roaring waters, the desires of many hearts a long while dead, bright wine in foaming cups, and blood precious as wine, and fierce hurting kisses and the influences of the stars. She was born, her mother said, under the influence of Mars, and for such a woman that is as bad as it well can be, for it means that she will have a deal to do with men. Some women, such as my Aunt Gudrun, would take no harm of this and might be born under the influence of all the stars in heaven yet nothing come of it. I am sure that if my aunt had been the only woman in a castle full of men she would have been safe. Those her face did not affright her tongue would. Yet it is an ill thing in me to jest upon the poor soul, with God now this long while, so I hope and pray, though ever and anon fearing it may be otherwise, for she was a very curst woman.

But Nesta was not thus. Men would be about her like bees, with their askings and their brawlings. She would be pale and weary from the burning of their eyes as a traveller too long in the sun of midsummer. She would have no rest of them till she was an old woman—if she ever won through to old age. I had knowledge of all this as I stood with her in the thicket of Christ-thorn, and I bowed my head as a beast before the butcher. When I looked on her, it filled me with wonder to see the whiteness of her alabaster turned rosy, as the tips of the day's eye. For I have looked on many saints and angels done in alabaster, yet never one of them turned all to rose like this one. But I knew it had pleased God to make a miracle. I desired to give her some great gift, but when I cudgelled my brain for a gift, behold, everything of time, and my living and dying, were less than one of the leaves of the wood-sorrel beneath her foot. And after a little longer it became such a hunger in me to give her something that I could not bear it, but tore open my wallet and took from it my charm which was a small flat bottle of Roman glass, of dim, sad-coloured blue, lapped in samite, containing seven tears of Christus. Now you will say, 'How came you, a poor nobody of a young knight, with seven of God's own tears, when the mighty and the rich would give their wealth for one?' I will tell you then that my mother, in her youth, was acquaint with Peter the Hermit, a very holy man that would do great things one day, I was sure, leading all the world to Galilee, calling them on through the groves of white oleanders, even to Gethsemane, and preaching to them so straitly that the very birds should come down out of the trees and confess their small sins; and kings be upon the ground all night, weeping; and in the morning, seeing from Heaven's wall that all peoples and nations and languages are here, in great expectancy, Christus Himself would come through the white oleanders and the world would suddenly crackle like broken ice, and Christus and the oleanders and all we poor creatures suddenly be in heaven. And partly this has come, though as yet only a part of the world has gone to Galilee, but the end is not yet. And those flowers that are to be translated with us all are not yet budded.

Now this Peter had a kindness for my mother, and when he had been for the first time to Jerusalem he brought her these tears in a scallop-shell. And she, fearing they would be drunk up by the air, put them into the blue flask from Virocon where the Romans lived, and gave it to me to keep me safe in Time and Eternity.

So I held out my seven tears of Christ to Nesta with a shaking hand, and she took them, smiling very graciously upon me.

'What is this little bottle?' she asked me, and I told her.

'Oh, it is magic,' she said. 'I am afeard. My mother has magic. She is of Merlin's line.'

'It is no magic,' I answered. 'It is to save you from all spells and witchen wiles for ever and ever.'

'But how came it that they could get as many as seven tears for one hermit,' she said, 'when there be so many hermits and also great Earls and Princes and Kings that would be fain of them?'

I answered her—

'It is because He wept so many tears. Can you wonder, in a world such as this? You mind how when He saw the young lord carried to burial that was his mother's only son, it says, "Jesus wept." And when you mind how many mothers are thus, and lovers parted, friends betrayed, and fair things trampled, you know that He must have wept a deal. When He turned and looked upon Peter, and when He said, "Hast thou been so long time with me and yet hast not known me, Philip?" I think there were tears in His eyne.'

'Will this little bottle,' she asked, with an anxious look, 'bring tears to me? I am afeard of it. I will bury it here among the wood-sorrel and make a mound of white stones and plant an acorn. And the tears will be at rest then. I greatly fear if I keep them they will bring me to some strait pass, and maybe I shall end a nun—and I would not be a nun,' she said, with those lips that were red as the fruit of the cranberry, and that voice of sweetest balm, 'I would not be a nun for a king's ransom! No! Why I should be scourged every day, for I do wrong as easy as I breathe, and whereas now the Lady Powis only whips me if she has the toothache or if her lord has clouted her, in nuns' housen you are beaten for the glory of God and without consideration of the toothache.'

7

I was filled with rage to think of her being beaten. It was like scourging a butterfly or defacing a statue of a queen.

'It is as God wills, what you are,' I said. 'We are His that made us. We follow His sweet piping up hill and down the cwms. If you are to come to nuns' housen and be beaten sore, it will only be because it is His will and wish. And you will stand higher in Heaven for it. But if you keep the little tears of Christ in your bosom, all will be well, in dark days or sunny.'

So she put the tear-bottle into her gown, and I thought how close it must be pressed between those white round breasts, and I was filled with a madness of lust to rest where the little bottle was. But Christ kept me.

'Lady,' I said, 'it is time to be going. Will you ride along with me, for I go to Powis also?'

She clapped her hands at that, for then and always she loved ease. So I whistled my horse and he came at a canter through the glades, nuzzling to my leather coat. He was the best horse ever I had, and came in direct line from the Conqueror's favourite.

We went at a gentle pace through the glade, where the running wind came not, save in the topmost twigs, where the green, quiet turf was all so still, spelled long ago and the key of the charm forgotten till Eternity.

'It likes me, this place,' said Nesta, with a grave look that made her face like a babe's.

'Why does it like you?' I questioned, but she would not say. Only she said:

'Holy. It be holy.'

It was holy. The May-lilies were budded in shelter, pearls on the green. I can never look upon May-lilies without calling to mind that day, and other days when we sought May-lilies. For I would never let Nesta go with any other to gather lilies, nor to gather nuts, nor go a-maying, nor fill her bowl with bramble fruit and cranberries. For there were many terrors in our country when I was young. There were the bands of freed or serfs, or serfs taking dog's leave. There were black Egyptians from over the sea and from foreign parts in Wales. There were the tall gaunt swine that would stand slavering at the edges of the forest, hating all things, and there were the pig-men, not much less lean and savage than their swine, and the pig-women, half naked, with long lank hair to the waist and sagging breasts like the udders of the hill cattle, who would catch a poor wandering maid and having stripped her sell her to some lord for a great price and buy swine. Wolves, also, there were, in the dells among the lily leaves waiting upon the evening and the dark, to devour my sweet love if she tarried long to pull the golden honeysuckle in autumn. There were wild ponies and deer at rutting time, and fierce wild cats and the large swans nesting in the pools in spring. I thought all things were prowling for my love, and sometimes in my youth I wondered mightily about God, Who had made all these lewd and bestial things, and had then made her, white as Eve's breast, and set her amid them. But now I see that His thought was to do this for my sake, that I should have joy of keeping her and saving her as well as might be.

'See now! The purple ones! Leave me pluck them!' cried Nesta, and she ran to a dell where grew the pale *viola canis*, that Virgil loved, and darker, fragrant ones.

'It wears on to evening,' I said. 'We must set forward.'

So she came, obedient, and held her posy for me, and then we rode softly on, through the remembering oaks and the yellowing garlands of mistletoe and through the witchen trees and the dark pines to Powis, saying few words, but those very sweet, and hearing, just as the drawbridge fell for us, scattered whinings of wolves in the waste places. Now Nesta must hasten to the side of the House Lady, for the knife was already in the meat and the mead foaming. And I saw that on Nesta's right hand was a dark knight, very subtle of eye, debonair and glib, and I hated him.

'Oh, sir!' cried Nesta, 'do not stand glum, but sit you here by me.' And graciously she made room on her left hand, yet I was not pleased, because he was there also.

'You be still mumchancing,' said Nesta, softly and slily.

'You have given him your right hand!' I said violently.

'Ah, but you have the heart side,' she replied.

She was ever quick in the uptake.

'Who is he?' I asked.

'He is the new Escheator that Rufus the King has sent to look about into all the wrong doings,' she said, 'and he is to dwell in a tall castle in a place they call Thurstan Bony.'

I was pleased at that, for the name was an ugly name, and, besides, the place had something unket about it, and I liked to think of him there, all alone, hearkening to the bodings of the owls.

I asked her his name and she said it was Ranulph Jorwerth. I hated the name as I hated the man, so you can see what a deal of labour God in His mercy had to spend on me, that I might do what I did in later days, even for his sake, Jorwerth's, the man I hated. And now that it is Our Lady's day, and spring drawing near, with great gatherings of starling in the reeds, evenings, and rosaries of buds in the ellum trees, it has come to me in a dream that I must hasten with my story, that I may finish it to the noble glory of God's Name. All is so fair, I never saw the leafless thorn so snowy-white outside our monastery wall. I never heard the merle and the mavis cry and whistle so sweetly, nor smelt such freshness of life in the wild gales. And He that was and is my friend has said:

'Look long on the apple-blow, for you will not see it agen. Listen well to the mavis, for come a year I shall have invited thee to my house. And leaning from heaven's wall you will see the white thorn shining deep down, like snow in summer, and you will hear the mavis sing so faint and far away that you must fill up the glats in the song from memory.'

So I am ware that, come another Easter morning, when my even-Christians give each other gifts at the Church door, I shall be away. For it is as at the Feast of the Birds in holy Italy—when the bell rings, the cage is opened, and the birds, joyfully arising, fly out by lattice or clerestory when they smell the heady air. And if some blunder and beat themselves upon the horn or painted glass, that is their own foolishness. Afore you, good gentlemen that read this say of mine, have even glimpsed the painted cover of it that I have made of vellum, with rich gold and vermeil, blue, white and ruddy, and a picture of Nesta in Our Lady's colours, I shall have heard the sudden bell, pealing through the brisk dawn, and laying down my quills and brushes, I shall hastily depart from this dark valley of Time, going out among the serried stars as a young knight bent on new conquest.

Now I pray you, good Christian men, have patience with me in this, that I speak so many and small things of one day, and have lived so many days that you will think—'If we notch a stick for all the days of his life and another stick for all his doings on one day, and add each to each, it will be so much as cannot be contained in any book or scroll.' It is because that being the first day that ever I met Nesta, it shineth and I see it clearer than most. And also I have great joy of remembering the past, having been hindered of it by the command of His Holiness and by my own resolve, as penance, for above sixty years. And now that in so short a while I shall be along with her and she a bright angel, winged like the seeds of sycamores, the old sickness of heart is not with me. Such a small time has the hour-glass to run afore she will call me, as many a time she did of an evening at Polrebec, opening her window of horn and calling through the silver air in silver voice—

'Gilbert!'

Aye. She will call Gilbert. But it will not be to the orchard of crab-apples and russets that we shall wander, but to the harbours of vines all traced with fruit of eternity, and forests of sweet apples grafted in Eden, and bullace trees and sloe trees with no sours in their fruit at all, which will be a great marvel, for indeed here upon earth they are very shrewd eating.

Now then, I linger on that long gone day, as the swallows will linger about the thatchen roof where they made their nesses in summer weather.

There was much talk and laughter in the great hall, and great plenty of food—deer's meat, hog, beef, besides birds of all sorts and a swan for the high table, stuffed with mulberries from an old tree in the castle yard. For though the castle was new, and not a patch on the old castle that had stood so long, they had left the mulberry tree that was planted by Roman hands. On the trestles of our table was a fine covering of the new-fangled fulled cloth, whitened in the meadows under Scrobbesbury walls. For Lady Powis was ever forrard in buying new inventions and she was also house-proud.

The Justice of the Forest and the Lord Forester of Salop were there, and had a deal to say to me about the King's hayes, which as most folk know are woodland places fenced in with stakes and wattles for keeping in the roebuck, and in Salop the King has two or three, one being in my demesne, on the Hill of Lyth. For I held Lyth and Conder and Hundeslit—that some call Stapleton—and Frodsleye and Werentenhale and Cotardicote. They said Jorwerth was to look very close into all these things, for the King thought there should be a deal more game than there was, and it would go hard with any lord of land on which a haye was situate, if it was found that the villeins or Welshmen had been making glats in the wattles.

For this they love to do. First they make a glat, then a tuthree go into the haye, going about the deer and driving them to the glat. Then the men outside, with arrows and spears and stones, slay them as they come. And in the evening in many housen is feasting at the King's expense. But I think it is the Welshmen and not the villeins nor the radmen that do this, for Welshmen are as crafty as Normans, and they would liefer get a thing roundabout for themselves than have it a gift straight forrard.

I said so to the Justice of the Forest at supper. But the Lord Forester of Salop nudged me with his elbow, saying:

'You speak overloud.'

Sure enow, he, Jorwerth, was staring and glowering upon me, like some coiled dragon covered in gold. For his coat of chain-mail was all gold and he had come too hastily in to do his armour off before dinner. What with all this gold, and his face of golden-brown from many suns in France and his rich eyes dark with gold in them, like deep fruits in burning lands, he had a kind of splendour about him that makes me think now of the word *opulentus*, but did not then, for then I had little Latin. Still, I could see very well that he was a man used to have all his will, and quickly. Only he would never lunge after it as I did. Nevertheless, he would get it. I judged him not an ill man, but not

11

a good man neither. God was not there, so into the house of his soul any strayed devil limping home to hell might lodge for as long as it might please him. And whether he became a great man, valorous in sin, or a mean man, pecking about at little sins here and there, would be according to the devil he lodged. For some devils can make a man mighty as Ulysses, and there have been a good few kings and chief speakers in the moots who have ruled strongly and spoken great words only because they had a devil, being nothing in themselves. But at long last he will have them away to hell, even if they are kings of all the world. And it is great pity to see such high folk with devils, when you think what a king may do if he lodges an angel. Such were a many of our Saxon kings, and I think they will sit very nigh the hearth in the Moot Hall of heaven.

So, looking hard in the eyes of the man Jorwerth, over that fairest head on earth, I saw that he lodged a devil but was not otherwise evil.

'Wilt know me again, Saxon?' he asked me.

'Aye,' I made answer, 'I know you.'

He smiled a little, covertly, as was his way when he met any anger or mislike, replying:

'You say "I know you," Sir Gilbert Polrebec, as if you knew no good of me.'

'To know is to know, good or bad.'

'And I, in my turn, know you, Polrebec,' he made answer, 'with your blue eye, true Saxon, cold as your frozen pools in the forest.'

Nesta lifted her eyes to his dark face, and he stooped to her as any man must to such magic.

'They bin no frozen pools, Lord Jorwerth,' she said, 'they bin April skies, to my seeing.'

Jorwerth bowed his head and sighed a bit, underbreath, but smiled as if not caring, and with his easy courteous way, which have all Normans, whether lords or barons, friars or abbots, he answered:

'Lady, let it be as you will. If you say he hath green eyes, green are they ever. If you say he hath a cast in one, woe betide who says anything else. If you say April skies, so be it, but April skies are not always fair.'

But seeing me scowling, Powis, who had a kindness for me ever, yet durst not go agen the King's Escheator, called out in his great bull's voice, that had given him the nickname 'The Bittern':

'How now, lords dear, let us have no hard words nor looks. Let us pledge each other in the bowl.'

For he was afeard there might be a brawl, such as happed all too often in a land of Christen men since the Normans came, so that it was a thing to return thanks to God for if the feast did not end with spilt mead, and scattered bowls, and great lords in all their fanglements snarling among the rushes on the floor with the wolf-dogs, their thumbs in each other's gullets.

Looking at my face, all red, doubtless from foolish rage, Powis laughed out. When he laughed, all that heard leapt as at a sudden attack by night, with the curses of men and horse-hooves beating and the flame of pine torches smiting on the dark. His foes, times, had been so feared of his laugh, thinking it was some dragon come up from the sea, that they had fled without striking a blow. And Powis would come swaggering home, grinning from ear to ear, to think that because he laughed so loud God had given him the victory. But if he gained one way he lost another, for the wenches were mortal afeard of him, and they would scream and start at his laugh and durst not have him for a lover, saving Lady Powis, a doughty woman afeard of neither God nor devil, much less of a lungeous laugh, but only fearing to have an empty meal-bin and not enow of dried meat for winter, and less flagons and bowls and tablecloths than other ladies. So she swallowed the laugh and the man and all, and if he beat her, she beat the tiring-woman, and all was peace.

The ways of women were always more of a mystery to me than the ways of God, so I never inquired why it was that, when Powis had smitten her upon the cheek, she should hate the serving-woman and love Powis. Nor did I question why Nesta, when she had said so sweet a thing of me, should turn her back on me and speak with Jorwerth.

'Lady,' he said, 'since I can see that you are neither Norman nor Saxon, tell me whence you come, of what lineage you are, and what is your heraldic sign?'

'I come from the Cymru, sir,' she made answer, 'and my home is in the waste; and my lineage is elf-lineage, and for our sign, it is a churn-owl with a kingly crown upon his head.'

As she spoke them in her honey voice, the words were strange past telling.

'Where, then, is this waste situate?' asked the Escheator, eager as men are when a thing touches their own special business.

'Sir,' she made answer, 'it lies betwixt Salop and Radnor. It lies also between life and death. It is betwixt and between all things.'

13

'Is it in Doom Book?'

'Nay, my lord, for it is in neither county. Nor is it in any hundred, nor does it pay geld.'

'How comes that?'

'Why, lord, it is faery ground and you cannot measure it nor go round it, for though it is only a narrow piece, times, of the width of three horses head to tail, yet, times, it will widen to eternity and yet again it will shrink to a knife-edge.'

'A very untoward country.'

'Aye, sir, very unket. You cannot put it in your books.'

'And your lineage?'

'It is from Merlin, lord. The family is bad to thwart. Our land is faery copyhold.'

'And your crest? What is the bird?'

'Know you not the churn-owl, sitting weaving spells all night on a bough, and flying like a flittermouse, and having his voice in one place and himself in another, so that you can never be sure of him?'

'And what is his crown?'

'He had his crown from the people of the waste for what he did when Arthur came. On a night of summer it was, and all so still, each drop of dew on his own twig, none falling, and Arthur came, with all his valiant knights, blowing a bugle at set of sun and taboring upon the door of our castle of Betwixt-and-Between. Then all the people in the castle put their pale faces close to the slots of the windows, crowding with burning eyes, crying out "Hai!" and "Och!" and "Ffwrdd!" which means, "Avaunt," and beating upon the walls with soundless hands. For if King Arthur made the sign of the Cross, the place would fall in like an o'er-blown rose. But just as Arthur lifted his right hand with Excalibur to make a Cross upon the air, the little lych-fowl, that is the churn-owl, fled at him in the dusk, and beat about his head, and called up his fellows to do likewise, keeping up such a whirring noise of spinning in the air, and always with their voices in one place and themselves in another, that at last the King grew perplexed and moithered and forgot his errand, for the noise of the churn-owl became for him the noise of Guenevere's spinning. This is the manner of this bird, to let make its song into the heart's desire of the listener.

'Then they all went softly away and never came back, and it is said Arthur never recovered of that drowse, and fell asleep at last in Cornwall.'

But, by this, Powis could keep back his laugh no more.

'If you hearken to Nesta, my lord,' he said, 'you'll never be your own man agen. Tales! And a honey-tongue the wench has, to cheat the King's Escheator.'

And seeing that he had made a jest to last for ever, he roared till the wolf-dogs bristled down their spines and filled the hall with howls.

'And would you indeed cheat the Escheator, lady?' inquired my lord. 'It goes hard with such.'

And, just for as long a time as it takes a sand grain to fall through the hour-glass, I saw his devil in his eyne. It was a wild-cat devil, and it gave an untoert snarling appearance to his young face—for he was not so much older than I, only his authority set its mark on him. I have seen him, care-free, shooting at a mark or playing at ball with Nesta, look a very lad.

But at most times he was an ill man to cross, and a hard man to dispute with. That is, if he would dispute. Mostly he would not. Nor did he speak much, in especial when deeds were afoot. When my father or the Earl of Powis would be roaring and shouting with the joy of coming battle, he would be as still as a snowman. With him, the wink of an eye oftentimes meant a man's death and a nod fired a township.

His voice, when he was in his glib moods, was an omen to all, it was so dark and slippery, like a slow-worm in the grass. He could say 'Give you good den!' in such fashion that you felt his long, well-shapen fingers about your throat. He could say 'God rest you!' and say it in pleasing voice, even as sweet as a church-singer singing in a miracle play, and yet you were stabbed to the heart.

You would think him a simple hernshawe, scarce fledged, but you would find as I found to my undoing and yet to the glory of God, that he was no hernshawe in his heart though he seemed one, but he was in truth a very old heron in his thinkings. For an old heron will never miss his fish. He will stand a-dream and simple-seeming, but let some good fat fish come by, he strikes, and the poor fish is no more. That Nesta was ware of this I knew because I heard him ask her—

'If the Saxon's eye is an April heaven, lady, what is mine?'

And Nesta lifted chin—ah! sweet chin, pearly rounded and somewhat pointed—and lifted her flower-face on its long slender throat (God will pardon me my words of Nesta, for has not our Father the Pope given me leave to put all that happed into my say, and it happed that Nesta was a very fair woman) and she made a measurement of him in her heart and she said—

'O my lord, to look in them wilders me. I see a dark forest, still and noon-hot, and o'er-topping rocks of red stone, burning with no sound, and, in the black leavy deepness of the boughs, wild cats prowling, gold, with golden eyes.'

'Nesta Llanvihangel,' said Lady Powis of a sudden, 'you talk too much. I see you bin fain of a whipping. To bed with you now, wench.'

So Nesta must leave the hall with speed, and go into the women's bower that was under the stairs, which were made very broad and twisting, of chiselled stone. For the man who made the pictures of the castle or ever it was built, had done none but poor barons' castles and burgesses' housen afore, and he was so heart-proud to be making noble steps of stone that he gave them a deal of room; and Powis had ever such a throng about him, of varlets and men-at-arms, kitchen men and gleemen, huntsmen, and hawks and dogs and a meiny of falcons (with this new little one from the land of the Gael westward and that new great white one from Norway) that he had much ado to bestow them all in the castle as it was then. In these latter days I hear that they have builded it to the size of the stairs, and it is a great place. But what Powis did then was to send the women under the stairs. There was but a curtain of tapestry afore the entrance, so I could hear right well the sound of the blows and Nesta crying out, saying:

'Ah! Ah! But there *be* wild cats in his eyne. Oh! leave be, leave be! I'll speak no more to the man!'

But Lady Powis was angered, to be sent to bed just when the gleemen came in, and she thwacked with a will, and I hated her sorely. But I saw by the darkening and dazzling of his eyne that Jorwerth liked her to be beaten, though he would lief have beat her himself, for already he lusted after her. But now it was time to listen to the gleemen because it was Powis's courtesy to have them in for us.

'Way there for the lord's gleemen!' shouted the porter, and in they came, swaggering in their ivy-coloured doublets and their long hose which he had gotten for them in London Town. They stood abashed to see so many lords and barons, and bowed low, doffing their round purpled hats and taking the opportunity to scratch their heads.

'Well, fellows,' said Powis, 'what will you sing?'

'We will sing what my lord wills,' said the chief gleeman.

'And suppose I will what you have no knowledge of?'

'Why then, lord, we must sing another tune or guess at it.'

16

'If you can guess my riddles, I'll leave you choose your own tune,' says Powis. ''Twas these riddles I wanted the women away for.'

All the gleemen stood agog, like dogs on the scent.

'What is it a woman hath till you have her?'

But at this Jorwerth, having observed the Lady Powis shaking her fist from the bower under the stairs, said—

'Let us have the songs first, my lord, an you will.'

'Shall we sing the Song of the Beautiful Persons?' asked the head gleeman.

'Sing what you please,' said Powis, vexed that his riddle was spoilt.

'Lords, lordlings and ladies beyond the curtain,' said the gleemen all together, 'we will now sing the Song of the Beautiful Persons.'

Then each lifted hand and they sang, some high, some low—

'Why were they born so beautiful,

Why were they born so cold?

Little Jesus was not beautiful in manger,

Nor Mary in fold.

But the beautiful o'erlooking strangers

Have taken our hearts in hold.

O why were they born so beautiful,

O why were they born so cold?'

And though that night the gleemen sang many songs, none lingered in my mind as that one did, for it seemed to speak my heartache. So I asked the gleemen, as they wiped the sweat from their faces, for they had sung very lustily, where they found that song, how they came by it and what it was. But they could not tell. Only they said it was a very old song, and some said, it was from Babylon and brought by the tin-men that came mining in Cornwall.

'That cannot be,' I said, 'for our Lord Christ was not born nor thought of then, nor was Our Lady.'

'Maybe they put them in after,' said the gleemen, 'but the other is from Babylon or further, and the tune also.'

Then the Sheriff, who was a man of some learning, being able to spell out the Paternoster in a Missal, said that he had been told it came from the East, where people made all of gold, fair and very cruel, with long eyes like spear-slits, dwelt beneath the sunrise, nourishing themselves on ghostly food and on blood, so that to live a thousand years was nothing to them, and every day they lived they grew more cruel in their thoughts and more beautiful in their countenances.

After the Sheriff spoke, the mead went round and the gleemen sang again till the night was far spent. Then Powis and such of us as were nobles retired to the sleeping chamber, and the rest lay down among the dogs.

In the morning we went hawking and I had no sight of Nesta till even. Only as we rode to the forest, passing near the oak-glade I saw afar the thicket of Christ-thorn and the sparse gold of the fading mistletoe, and I mused on her and on all fair things. And I thought she would not like to see the poor stag torn, and I was minded how Christ made a miracle in Gothland.

There was a young huntsman there, as it might have been I that speak, and he was so set on his sport that his heart became cruel. But on a day, when he had galloped hard after his stag, and was about to kill it, the stag turned, neither spent nor breathed, and looked softly upon him, and there, behold! he saw the Cross of Christ in light upon its brow. And humbly kneeling on his knees he said—

'O little stag! I see thou hast the Lord, and if thou hast, all have, and it pitieth me to think how many times I have slain Christ.' And he left chasing the deer from that day on and became an anchoret. Now it seemed to me that there was somewhat for me in this old tale, and thinking on it I turned aside from the hunt and rode softly through the grove. Then it was as if a hand was laid upon my heart and a whisper was in my ear, and I knew it was God dealing with me, calling me out from the world. So being but just come into the glory and hey-day of the world since I saw Nesta, I was lief to keep it and I was feared of the solemn grove where all was a-whispering—

'Christus natus est.' So, putting my horse to a gallop, I caught up with the hunt.

Now what we did on this day we did every-day, and it was all pleasant to me, so that I was as one of those men who have from time to time fallen through into faery, and heard the singing of the birds of Rhiannon and forgot himself. So I stayed even till Easter drew on, courting with Nesta and hardening my heart agen the dealings of the Lord, who seemed to become more urgent with me as spring drew on, giving me no rest. He would touch me on the shoulder when I leaned over the drawbridge to jest with the scullion wenches washing themselves in the moat, and He would say, inside my heart, 'Not that way, boy. No day-spring is there.'

And He seemed to be willing me to some great undertaking, yet would not tell me forthright, being liever I should guess His riddle. But He was urgent with me, and when I lay a-listening to Powis his snores with my thinkings full of Nesta, He would begin of it, and when I fell asleep, He sent visions of the night.

Now I will tell you one of my visions:

I saw a great hollow sandy place, such as conies love, rounded and broad and sloping upward to the sky, higher than a castle. And conies were there, and martlets, with their young safe housed in the holes of the warm banks, and a fox slunk by. Then came a voice hollow and grievous, a harsh voice, yet winning.

And it said—

'Foxes bin safe in earth, martlets bin hid in sand-hole, but the bright lordling of Eternity and His Mother have no lodging. They bin far spent with wandering, and they want their house in Galilee. Who will ride along of me to win back their litel house in Galilee for the lordling Christ and His Mother? They bin so tired, dear folk, and their feet hurt, and they cry in the night. You may hear the crying in all trees, and about the eaves, and in the space of the roof, where the smoke goes out.'

All the while the voice came nearer, and then across the sandy place there came a man. A very big man he was, but thin as a scarecrow. His legs were bare to the thighs and he was clad in a wolf-skin. As he walked, he swung his arms like flails or sickles, as if there were so much power in him that he must ever swive the empty air. The power of the man was such that when folk saw him, straightway they began to do as he did, striding with heads thrown backward and eyes looking into the far away, and flailing with their arms.

After the man came a crowd of people great enough to fill the sandy place in every part; so that the flat place even to the steep sides was nothing but faces, close as salted trout in a tub. The conies scuttled to their burrows and the martlets knew not what to make of it and fled here and there with cries, whilst their babes came to the thresholds of their nesses to see what might be, and stayed with their innocent faces crowded together, and their white chins packed one above another, to hear Peter Hermit.

How great was the multitude, and of how many differing folk! Rich merchants in gowns of scarlet velvet-stuff with round furred hats, white nuns and black nuns, pig-women and women of the town, sinfully bedizened, and great ladies in gowns of clear-coloured sendal with ermine and squirrel furs.

* * *

One day I went to the armourer and asked him to make a small ring out of a lump of silver from Cotardicote, and to put in it the purple water-clear stone my mother brought in her dower and gave to me, and to engrave inside the ring. So he asked what words. And I said—

'I love thee.'

'Oho! my lord, if it is thus and thus, I will make the ring the best that I can, but you must get me a writing of the words to go by.'

'Where can I get that?' I asked. 'From the Sheriff, think you?'

'No,' he said. 'The Sheriff can spell out other men's letters but he cannot make any of his own. Best ask the monk.'

'Where shall I find him?'

'In the small anchorhold of wattle that hangs upon the wall of the castle above the Earl's enclosed garden, like the nest of a canbottle.'

So I waited till owl-light, being abashed, for love was new, and I came to the holy father as he was saying his paternosters. He was a white monk, and his great hood of white woven stuff stood out far about his face, shadowing it and making it seem little and withdrawn, white within white, as the mid of the cuckoo-pint glimmers, far in, cased and folded in its cerements. The holy father held up his long bony hand and made know that I must kneel till his say was done. It irked me to meet thus again with God, for I was willing to avoid this path. I was as a man who has not paid his tithe, and seeing the tithe man coming down a ride of the woods he will turn aside and go by a roundabout way. Yet in the end he mun pay his tithe.

While we knelt there, darkness came stealing like a wolf, and the father's face went further into his hood till I thought he had been lost to this world.

'Son,' he said, when he arose, 'the Lord hath need of thee.'

So there in my path again was the tithe man, and I could never escape him.

'You came, little son, to offer thee to God?'

'No, father,' I answered roughly, 'but to ask of thee a posy for a ring. And a posy for a ring I will have,' I shouted, stamping about the room like an unbroken colt. 'No hoods to make my face little and grey and far within, like yours, old man! I say, I'll have a posy.'

'Well, well, son,' he replied peacefully, in his end of evening voice, 'and what posy had you in mind?'

So I hung my head and told him.

'I love thee,' he repeated. 'Well, son, if you are come to the stair "I love thee," you be not far from the topmost rung of the ladder. For this "I love thee" is like the rolling ruddy sun that drags in his wake clouds of all colours, warmship, flocks of doves, showers of blossom, dews in hid places, and the scatter of curlew-song, like broken tear-bottles.'

He looked upon me as it were mockingly a while.

'You are a cunning one, boy,' he said, 'for it seems but a little posy, yet in it you seize the whole world and put it into the small roundness of your ring. Now, how shall I write this posy?'

'Oh, in pleasant letters, father, and flourished a little.'

'Pleasant they will be, for the thing written formeth its own letters. Flourished, you say, and so you show me that the brothers and sisters of poverty are not yet acquaint with you. For that flourished is of the world, and consorts with folk at tourneys, and saddles of Persian leather, and cap-feathers, and heraldic signs done in gold and silver.'

I could think of nothing to say, save to blurt out:

'She is very fair.'

'Yes, son. She is very fair, and if the dear Mother pleases that she find her soul, she will be a great angel one day. She is as golden as orchards of the Hesperides, and nought of darkness in her. Give her a soul and you have enriched heaven. Yes, lad, we must put in the flourishes.'

'I thank you kindly, father,' I said, and turned to go.

'Kneel while I bless you'—and he held out his hand, long and pale, and spoke fast in the Latin tongue that sounded gibberish to me, and it seemed to me that it was less like a blessing than a spell—as if he would put God's charm on me and so lime me for heaven. And as I went out into the softness of night, his dim, withdrawn eyes followed me, mocking kindly, as a mother mocks her climbing babe, so unruly, so high-stomached, going here, going there—but see, all the while the mother's arms are about him.

Coming out of the garden in the dusk, I saw the forest stand up like a dim curtain of Bayeux, with here a vasty oak and there a clump of ellums, and every burgeoning tump of trees was like the boss of a shield, so that it seemed some lady had embroidered this curtain with the bossed shields of a great army.

I could hear Powis going the round of his hawks and merlins, for it was the feeding hour, and he would have none feed his hawks but himself. I could hear through the open door of the house-place the whirring of the six spinning-wheels of Lady Powis her maidens. And looking through the small bow window where a page had cut an eye-hole I could see Nesta, jimp and small in her silk robe, yet lily-tall, stooping over the embroidery she was working on for her mistress. I knew what she was stitching—a knight in armour, silvern like mine, not golden like Jorwerth's. Seeing her pale cheek and golden hair bent so sweetly, I thought, 'Now she has no ring, but come three days she will have her heart's desire.'

Then a great seething of love began in me, so my heart was like to burst and I was glad when one of the dogs lifted muzzle and howled, for it seemed he howled for me, to ease me. So I went in, and Nesta looked softly on me and asked me:

'Why did the dog howl so? They do not save at night.'

She asked it, as she ever did, as if I being all-wise could tell all.

So I laughed and said maybe I had put a spell on it to howl for me.

Then she said eagerly:

'My father could make all the dogs howl at Tochswilla whensoever he chose.'

'Where is Tochswilla?' I asked.

'It is our castle, whither I shall soon return.'

'No!' I cried out. 'Never will I let you go.'

'Nobody may keep a maid from going home-along, sir.'

I caught her hand with the needle in it and drave the needle into my palm for joy of the prick of her needle.

'You have no ring!' I said.

'Only great ladies have rings.'

'But you desire to have a ring?'

'She knows well that a serving-woman's affair is not the wearing of rings and gems and cloth of gold,' said Lady Powis. But I smiled, thinking how I would give it to my love in the avenue of oaks in three days. And even so it was, which was cause for joy, since in this world things happen mostly other than our dreams. We dream sunshine and awaken to the wan light of owls. But that day came as I willed, and nought spoilt it. The armourer kept faith and did the ring, and I went to Nesta in the house-place and said:

'Nesta, I thought to take my horse for a gallop in the forest, to the oak grove where the road is clear. Oot come?'

'So will I!' she cried. 'Indeed to goodness it will be fine, this sweet April.'

So we rode away into a world of dreams, and the dreaming mistletoe still hung there, green gold, the oaks still called ancient things to mind, and the thorn that I found budded was white over.

'Oh, be we going to my bower?' she cried, in that delightsome voice which was as the springing of a thousand flowers. But I made no answer, for no words came. Only when we stood in the thorn-brake I took her small long hand and set the ring upon it, and kissed it, and kneeling set her hand upon my head. And after a while I got to my feet again and said, When would she come to Polrebec? But she only stood trembling and saying, 'Gilbert! Gilbert!' and looking at the ring as if she feared it.

'Why, by your looks, you might be an elf maid, feared of all Christian things!' I cried.

'And so it is,' she answered, solemn. 'For I come from elf housen, from the land of Betwixt-and-Between. I cannot thole a mortal bond. I am afeard. Yet I so love the ring, and thee.'

'But the ring first and most,' I said glumly.

She laughed at that, yet when I kissed her she shuddered.

'It would be best for me and thee,' she said, in a strange bewitched voice, 'best that I go back to Tochswilla. Nine old witch-women to tend the cooking-pot. Nine wizards to tend the fire. No commands to be given, no love to be given, nought to do or think or

23

feel. With thee, so much heart's joy, but sorrow and pain and anxious cares. The bread to make and manchets to apportion. Spinning and weaving and the ordering of the house.'

'My mother would do that, child.'

'Ah, but thy mother would not do the hardest.'

'What is it, then, my mother would not do?'

'It is thy love, Gilbert, it is lover's love I am afeard of. My clay likes it not. It is not altogether mortal clay, and nearness frights me.'

'Frights you? What are you afeard of?'

'I cannot tell. Some touch—something of grief—when your hand touches my hand, it saddens.'

'But then, you love me not at all,' I cried roughly.

'Ah! I love thee, Gilbert, as well as I may. But I would liefer not.'

'But would you be a maiden for ever, then, without husband or babes?'

'It is the fashion of our women to be so.'

'How then do you go on? How came you?'

'Oh, our menfolk go abroad for their wives. They are otherwise—more mortal. But few of our women wed, and when they do, they sup sorrow.'

'It is a great pity,' I said craftily, 'that you cannot have my ring, nor see the pleasant folds and scraps about Polrebec, nor ever walk in my litel grey garden.'

'What be that, Gilbert? The litel grey garden?'

'It is our castle-close at Polrebec. It hangs upon the wall like a nest, and the wall shelters it. There be grey stones to walk upon and bushes of grey lavender on either hand, with rosemary and thyme and hig-tapers—all grey of leaf. And the small-leaved, musky white rose, and two or three violets and many May-lilies under the wall. And on summer noons, when the land swelters, the litel grey garden is sweet and dim in the shadow of the wall. And I had thought to see you there, Flower of the West, spinning amid the drowse of the bees, gold in the grey.'

'Oh,' she cried out vexatiously, clasping her hands, 'you have made me fain of yon grey garden.'

'It is not worth your thoughts,' I said. 'It is but a poor garden. I will root it up. And the ring is nought. I will fling it into the brake. And never will you call me through the window of horn, saying, "Hey, hey, Gilbert! Collops bin cooked."'

'Oh, I am fain, I am fain of thy Polrebec, Gilbert,' she cried out. 'I will forget Tochswilla and the little witch-women and the little witch-men, I do love thee and thy litel grey garden and thy collops. I'll put no more stitches in for cross mistresses, a-pricking of my finger, and the tears falling.'

'What?' I shouted. 'Thou'lt come? Nesta, Nesta, thou'lt be Lady Polrebec, riding away with me to my own people?'

'Iss, fey, when I have made my wedding garment and made send from Tochswilla my chest and my casket. For though I be only a sewing-woman, I have stuffs of Arabia, with buds and flowers of pearl, and I have an ermine mantle, and a wimple made all as fine as cobweb. And in the casket is a shining brow-circlet with one great dazzling gem, and this we put on when we come to two score years, being still maiden.'

'Why not otherwise?'

'Oh, it brings ill. But none the less I shall wear it when I wed with thee. Oh, it is a brow-circlet fit for a queen. I shall shine so! Be there many people at Polrebec?'

'There is father and there is mother, and there is Aunt Gudrun.'

'Will they love me?'

'Mother will love thee. Father has little time for loving. Aunt Gudrun hath little love for giving.'

'Why has thy father little time?'

'Oh, because he has bad neighbours. He is lord of Stretton-in-the-Dale, but lives alone with me till he can gather enow of men to conquer his bitter neighbours.'

'And that Gudrun, is she a harsh woman?'

'A little. But none could be harsh to thee, lovely flower. Shall we ride, Nesta, shall we ride home?'

'In due season, Sir Gilbert the hurriful.'

'But when?'

'In May-month, when all is fair. Toward the ending of the month, for it will take a long while to send to Tochswilla. And, eh! how they will gibber and how they will mop! Oh, my soul, they will put a curse on me!'

'No! You have my little bottle. And now, see, you have also my ring, and within is a motto, very strong to save.'

Then she said, 'What be it?' for, like all women and most men, she could not read.

And when I told her, she said it in the voice of crooning cushats, and I eased my heart with a great bursting sigh, and kissed her, and set her on my horse, and so with an arm about her came back to Powis.

As soon as we were raught back, we saw beside the moat a train of pack-horses and asses and a brown woman from over the sea, an Egyptian, selling stuffs of Damascus to my lady Powis. So I thought it would be good sport to bid Nesta vie with her mistress for this and for that. Nor was Nesta long in seeing the jest, and knowing her mistress to be of a saving disposition and knowing that I had plenty of gold pieces in my coffers, she offered the woman more than Lady Powis for a certain piece of white Damascus linen, needleworked with lilies.

'How now, madam!' says Lady Powis. 'Since when are you a house-lady?'

'Only but now, mistress. Only since the shadow of Breidden slipped from Englefield Wood to Pigeon Meadow.'

'Waiting-women who make game of their ladies must be whipped,' said Lady Powis.

The gipsy smiled at me with a dazzle of white teeth in her oaken face, as if to say—

'End it, young man.'

So I said, 'Lady, Nesta buys for her own house, and I wear the Flower of the West from now onward.'

Then Jorwerth, standing idly by, frowned. For to a lord without booklearning, tied by the leg in some outlandish place by the king's order, a pretty gentlewoman is very passable sport. But, being a man quick in the uptake and of good address, he was the first to give Nesta his wish. But when he had wished her joy, he must twist the occasion to his humour, saying:

'Lady, I should wish to enforce the law that you must not sell to others what you have not first offered to the overlord.'

'Then, sir,' she says, peart as a robin, 'I will offer me to the King of Elfland, since he is the only overlord I will own to. And besides, I know he will not take me, since he has so many lights o' love with hair of spun silver and faces of pearl; so many lemans out of the water, smooth as lilies; so many sweet concubines from Arabia beyond the sea, whose kisses ravish the heart, whose breasts are painted with the soft colours of wild apples.'

'And what says Polrebec to that?'

'O Gilbert,'—she whispers—'Gilbert'—and could get no forrarder.

'From the King of Elfland and all other kings, from the Lord High Escheator of Elfland and all other Escheators,' I cried out, 'this short dagger and this long sword shall defend her.' And I held up the sword pointing skyward and the dagger longways, so they formed a cross.

'Ai! Ai!' cried out the gipsy suddenly, 'thou hast made a cross. And behold, it is thine own. It is the dukkerippen.' With that, she folded up her stuffs and put her money in her bosom, and without another word departed.

By this, Lady Powis had had time to get it into her head that she had no waiting-woman, but only a guest maiden about to be Lady Polrebec. So she made her go in to look at the purchases and to speak of bridal things and the linen and such like fardels. Then Powis clapped me on shoulder.

'Thank God,' he says, solemn as an owl, 'that you've gotten a plenty of good oak trees for cradles, young Polrebec.' He began to laugh, but checked.

'What of Gudrun?' he questioned. 'What of my old friend, eh? Ah, Gudrun and I—well, well. Old days! Aha! Well, lad, if thine aunt is hardfavoured, at least she is virtuous.'

And at last allowing his laugh to have its way, he departed to his purlieus, his favourite falcon (that he had of a Dane at the wharf of London, hailing from Iceland) sidling and hissing upon his wrist.

How shall I now tell of my thoughts of Nesta as I rode home-along in the fair green weather? I cannot find any words for them, and I must therefore tell you them by speaking of other things. For if a thing is too near us, so that we cannot get the measure of it proper, and if it is too dear, so that no word is bright enow, then it is best to tell of some other thing, and in telling of that we shall tell of the dearest thing, though in roundabout fashion, for at such a time we stamp the image of our one thought on everything. So, because I cannot tell of the whiteness and the fragrancy of the Flower of the West, I will tell of the may-blossom that foamed the land as I went singing home. Doubtless it would be a stern winter, for the haw-fruit would come so thick, seeing what the blossom was. But what cared I for winter? What thought had I, a young man promised to wed, with a good horse under him, gleeful and healthful in that pleasant *Now*, so long gone by? And how strange a thing it is that we feel in this *Now*, when it is pleasant, like a creature in a ball of crystal, safe housed and shut away. But when it is grievous, we say, 'The bubble *Now* is but water.' Yet if we think right, there is no *Now* or *Then*, no wall of glass or of water, no hour shut away, but all, whether sad or merry, spent in Eternity, there lapsing, there renewed.

'God bless the thorn!' I sang, and indeed it was blessed that year. The toppling brakes, that had made way wherever the forest gave back a little, were white as giant bridewomen. Down gentle hillsides, clad in the blackness of pines, came runlets and rivers of white. In bosky places beside the water it lay like cruddled milk. And in such places as Long Mountain, where they had ploughed linches along the hillsides, every linch had its scattered sentinels of thorn; in those underhill clearings where a gore acre ran up to a point in the woodland it was prinked out in white like the ermine on a lady's gown. I mind how at Pontesford above the mill was a great may-tree like the mercy of God, spread everywise, and doubled in the pool. I stopped there, letting my beast drink, and gathered a bunch of may for my hat, looking into the wonder of the whey-coloured blossoms with their centres of the rich rose of sword-tassels.

The miller looked out of the window-hole and hastened down to me with a piece of bread and bacon.

'Sir Gilbert's face is morning-bright,' says he. 'Hast found Roman gold at Cotardicote, Sir Gilbert?'

'No,' I said, 'but I've found a golden girl out of Wales, miller, and I'm promised to wed.'

'Oh, bin ye indeed, sir? And luck go with you! But by my best barley, it's a middlin' job, this wedlock. Look at me now! Take warning by me. I married.'

'You look to me in good case enough, miller.'

'I be so, lord,' says he, '*since I lost her*. God keep her!'

'Oh, you're a sore man, miller, a sore man for a joke,' I said, and, munching my bread and bacon, rode on. And the nigher I came to Polrebec, the sweeter grew the may. Of the tallness of three or four men it stood at the forest edges in the evening light, spelled by its own fragrancy. And if you shut eye to rest from the wound of its too much beauty, it rose with the evening breeze and buffeted you upon the brow. There is no escape from that which is beautiful. It will have our homage. Sometimes I have even been glad of summer's end to rest me. So swiftly the may treads on the heels of the daffodils, and folded roses be waiting even while the may burgeons, and woodbine stills the heart with a sigh, and then corn yellows in every scrap and gore of barleyland, and lo! apples bin ripe, all painted in one night by an angel. And methinks, times, it is great peace to turn away from all this lust of loveliness to the chilly call of winter, where is nothing to keep our thoughts back from Him. And then the spirit rests no more in this or that carnal thing of petalled delight, but starteth away hastily over the waste waters, like a seamew, plaining for eternity.

When I raught home in the rare light of even, my father was still ploughing the piece we called the old field. He had no belief in a lord of the manor sitting idle by hearth, and his say was ever that a foldworthy man should plough better than a radman. So we toiled and moiled right heartily, and I am sure no riding tenant nor villein in all the land ever sat down to his supper more sharp-set than we did. My father gave over ploughing when he saw me, and my two dove-grey oxen turned their brown eyes to look upon me. I did love these oxen, coloured like the grouse that fly about Mount Gilbert, from which bosky hill I was named.

'Well, boy,' says my father, 'you tarried a good while. You binna like the disciple that did outrun Peter. I doubt you'll think our sport poor after the boar-hunting and the buck-hunting and the hawking there, done all in the best manner.'

'Why,' I said, 'you know, sir, I'd liefer go after a badger with you than hunt the elk with the King of Faery.'

My father chuckled a bit.

'Well, well,' says he, 'I doubt I binna cut out for a faery; I bin too fat.'

He wiped his face with his arm and breathed heavily, for he had more blood in him than he knew what to do with, and in the spring of the year and the fall of the year my Aunt Gudrun put leeches to him. For she was wise in such things and knew a deal about herbs and simples, though I used to think she made her potions more noxious than need be. And she would watch the sick one swallow it with such a look, as if to say, 'I'll learn ye to be took sick.' And if anybody was in need of the Mass-thane to give Extreme Unction, she would flounce about the place as if the poor soul had done it to spite her and she would say to us in the house-place—

'There's Welsher's wife now, taken with a hoost. Her means dying'—as if we were to blame.

'I went a-hunting only a few days,' I said, 'and those were the days I liked least.'

'By Thor and his black lambs,' said he, 'what May games have you been playing? When a young fellow gives over hunting, there's mischief brewing. Come Daphne, now, come Felelolie! Day's done.'

As we came home with the oxen following, looking largely upon us with their brown eyne, I could see my mother from afar, in the litel grey garden. For my castle stood high, on a round pyatt, so from the garden you could see all and be seen by all.

'I'll tell thee, father, of my May games when we are set down to supper. I have a deal to tell.'

'Well-a-day, I hope the news is good news,' he said, 'for I must tell you, son, the marbled stallion means dying. I found him up in the beanland chumbling young bean sprouts, the fool. Seems as if the beasts are bewitched when you bin away. This one plotting to take sick and that one planning to break pasture, and nobody to do a hand's turn.'

'Not Aunt Gudrun?'

'Oh, Gudrun. Ah. She's very forrard in helping, is Gudrun. She went after the brindled cow that strayed on to Cotardicote, but she made such a belownder that the cow did drop her cauf. And as nice a little cauf it would ha' bin as ever I see.'

'Well, father, it is the will of God and we must stomach it. I'll go see to the glats in the wattle to-morrow.'

We came to the gate of the castle, and there was my mother, looking just what she was, a very dearworthy woman, a good woman and fair, but not in any wise clever as men are clever, only strangely visited by angels at times, who told her things unknown to other folk. So now she never hiver-hovered at all, but looked at me bright and quick, saying, 'Who be she, Gilbert, my son?'

'She is the Lady Powis her waiting-woman,' I answered, as if she had said some daily thing, for we were used to her ways.

'What standing has her father?' asked mine. So I said she had none, but came from Tochswilla, twixt Salop and Radnor.

'Tochswilla!' cried out Aunt Gudrun. 'Necromancy!'

'And what of her mother?' mine asked.

'She is dead. Nesta hath no strength of people about her.'

'Nine witch-women, she has,' cried Aunt Gudrun, 'and nine witch-men, and they maken simples, unguents and nards enough for all the queans of the world. And they sell them not for lumps of gold nor pearls, but for unhallowed things—gibbet-men, twyheaded puppies, green plants that spring with leaves raddled with blood—and worse things.'

'It was a hold of Merlin's once,' said my father. 'And you can always know a hawk's nest by the strawn feathers. There is a strangeness in all Merlin's places, hereabouts or abroad, as Conway.'

'But is the maid a bad maid, then?' mother asked me. 'Is she chrissen maid?'

'I know not if she is chrissen, mother, but she is no whit bad.'

'Neither bad nor good,' quoth Gudrun, and snapped her wide mouth like a prison portal.

'Hath she said anything of housewifery, son?'

'Why, not so much, mother.'

'Well, it is not so bad as might be,' father said. 'He might have brought us a gipsy or a light-o'-love, or a villein's wench, or a woman from London. And this one hath a certain nobility. Thwarted and twisty, but yet it is nobility. It would have irked me otherwise, for I am a man in a good position, albeit troubled with enemies, and I can pay my tax sesters of honey for many more hunting horses than I need, and I can pay also my tribute of corn and beer and sheep and food-rent to Rufus for fifty men for a day and a night and a day. If I am here in my lad's little castle, it is no disgrace to me, it is only that about my castle of Stretton-in-the-Dale there be too many ill-wishers.'

'What was her mother's name, son?' my mother questioned, not noticing father, since he ever spoke thus when a thing stirred his mind.

'Fernella, mother, was her name.'

'A strange, God-forsaken name,' cried Aunt Gudrun. 'I shall mislike the girl.'

'A bowl of mead!' my father shouted, 'and let all the servants come and drink to Lord Gilbert's health, and wish him long life and a good bedfellow and many sons to fight against his enemies. Benedictus benedicat!'

So came I home, and knelt that evening to look upon the Stiperstones hill through the window of horn that would open, and never in life had the purple hill or the burgeoning forest or the bursting blossom of the orchard seemed so fair and so blessed. God be with all us poor men whom He leads in ways undreamed, making darkness for day, winter for spring, silence for music, till all bemused and dumbfoundered we fall upon our knees, crying, 'Where bin my Father?'

I found a mort of work to my hand, for we kept no riding-tenants, and all was to do for father and me and a few villeins. What with the wattle fences, and the beanland and barleyland, and our big scraps of cleared land for herds, and the keeping of the haymeads in watch and ward, which must be done the summer through, till Lammas, a man had not much time to be love-sick, albeit in his dreamings he might go a-homing to her that was the painted lanthorn of his life.

Now behold! I was in the beeves' field, and my dearworthy Lord stood beside the sheepcote. He bin so wise, He bin so knowing, He was ware that my heart was all furrowed and scrat with love, as our fields with the plough, and He took thought to sow His own seed there.

'Gilbert Polrebec,' quoth He, and His grey eyne were keen upon me as hawks flying agen a stormy sky, 'Gilbert, me wanteth for lack of thee. There bin a glat in my array of men, Gilbert, and I cannot set down Lucifer, who was once my own house-carl, and has taken arms agen me, if there is any place where he may come in. For he knoweth the ways of the house, and such foes are the worst foes. Come forrard, then, Polrebec, with all your strength, to my aid. Lukka! When Rufus calls up his men, offering threepence a day, twenty thousand spring up in a se'nnight. Gilbert, I do not offer thee a poor threepence, though as this world goes it is good enough pay. But I have offered thee a lordship in Eternity, bigger than a Cornish acre, richer than barleyland or beanland—a seat at my hearth and a slumber-place at the foot of my own bed. If I could do more, I would do more. But you mun serve me now. Would you be a Monday-man, idling six days of every se'nnight? Say not, "See, I have lost my love!" For I shall have her in guard. If you see her not afore, you will see her in heaven-town, coiffed and wimpled by my own mother. But thou canst not have her now, Gilbert.'

With that, I looked down at the beeves their field and up into God His heaven, and in the first I saw the coots playing about the pool, mating, and in the second, I saw the swans streaming over, mated.

So because I had no words, I pointed at them, saying—

'These, Lord?'

'It is their time,' He answered. 'Your time is not yet. In the spring that hath no autumn you shall wed with her.'

'But it is now, Lord, that my flesh burns and my ears pound at thought of her.'

'Natheless, you cannot have her,' He said. 'Her folk are not my folk. Her soul was all pied and streaked with evil while yet she was a poor babe in cradle. It is a great ransom must be paid for her.'

'All I have, master, save only enough to keep a roof over the old folks and enough of mead in the butt, and meal in the box while they live.'

'It is not enough, Gilbert.'

'What would you then, master?'

'Thou art the ransom, my son.'

Then turned I away a little for fear of meeting those eyne, grey-misted as the spinneys at dawn, with lights in them of the colour of hyacinthus. For I had heard tell that in the candles of His eyne you might see Calvary in little. And seeing it, all else was lost. And when I turned once more, He was vanished away, and only the spent blackthorn bush trembled in the light.

I mused a long while upon this, that He should come so to me, a poor cotman of His kingdom. Then, of a sudden, a tempestuous wind arose, roaring in the forest on every side, so that I must yell to my oxen in the dung-cart, yet could they scarcely hear, for the mighty voice was speaking with the voice of victorious armies—

'The Lord hath need of thee.'

So when I raught home, and was sitting by the fire of pine-logs, eating my manchet and drinking my mead, watching the blue smoke wavering up through the roof-hole to the patch of sky, blurred with a few stars, I asked my father what this vision could be.

And he said, 'It is the sickness out of the marishes. Gudrun must fettle you.'

So Gudrun put leeches on me, but yet the vision lingered, and mother said, 'Thus and thus was the vision shown to Peter Hermit in his fourteenth year, in a woodland bordering on the sea, hung with golden globes, as altar lamps, and all still as a spell in a hot seethe of sunshine, with shadows black as cowls. By which we see that in the Northland and the Southland, in silence or noise, He speaks but the one message, and He will not be denied.'

'Benedictus benedicat,' said my father. 'Pour me more mead!'

For he wearied soon of religious talk, saying it made his head ache worse than a cudgelling, and would lie upon the settle, breathing hard and closing up his eyne, while Gudrun poured cold water upon him, as he were some wizard burning on the witchen fire, suddenly spoke for by an angel and so swiftly douted.

* * *

33

Now these visitations came but seldom, for what with the farm work and hunting and father's ill-wishers we were hard put to it to get time enow for our work between the day-spring and the curfew bell—for I had sent for a little bell to London, and had put it in the small turret, and it did cause much searching of heart amid the owls and the stars which had nested there. Now was the time when all the forest folk brought forth their young and so grew bold, and here would be a lamb gone at dusk, when the slinking wolf was abroad, and there would be one of our tame lag–geese gone to the fox, doves to the falcon, and our mares breaking pasture, hearing the shrilly neigh of the sires of the wild horses upon the high places of the hills. And I was glad, for all this chivvying to and fro kept Him away, who in my thoughts was become ever as my chief ill-wisher, the marauder of my life, and the falcon marking down my dove. Late and early I was about, so that our shepherd was astonished, seeing me pass by the sheepcote afore dawn, and the ox-driver bringing out his team at break of day found me already there and the work half done.

Now I was up on Long–mynd, looking for estrays afore light on a dewy May morning. Wild ponies moved upon the rim of the hilltops against the sky, the grouse laughed above their nesting-places like merry wizards, and to walk across the hill-top was to wade in water.

I turned west, where, in the light of coming dawn, I could see Breidden, that lordly twinned mountain, standing sharp and dark on the silver of eternity. There was Powis, and my love sleeping. Suddenly a compulsion was on me, as if one said—

'Turn eastward.'

So I turned my back on Powis and looked beyond Caradoc to the rim of plain and the sky lightening as if one lifted a lanthorn out of sight. And as I looked I saw a most strange showing of God's power. For the blue rim turned to gold, as sea-beaches, and against the dawn, small but very clear, stood trees such as we have not in our country. They were most like big turnip-tufts at the top of lances, very tall and fearsome to see.

So I fell upon my knees, which is meet before a miracle, saying my Paternoster with closened eyne. And when I opened them agen, see! all was as before—Mount Gilbert, and Ercall, and the low rim of the plain like a bowl.

'It is some evil wile,' I said in my heart. But then a quiet voice made answer, 'No. It is Holy Land.'

And indeed, as I found after, so it was, and I had my first sight of Galilee amid the may-blossom, and in my early years this seemed a thing to astound a man. But now it doth not, for if He could firstly call together dust out of the air, star fragments, thunder-bowts, and compound them into the solid world, and call up the seas, that must in sooth have taken a deal of gathering, rain-drop by rain-drop—if, I say, He could maken

34

all these things in the first days of creation, what a litel thing it must seem to Him to make a small picture of Galilee 'twixt Ercall and the further hills.

'O Lord!' I said, 'thy showings be too hard for me.' And greatly fearing that there would be another, I ran whome as fast as might be.

* * *

But now came on the wedding morn, and I must ride, with all my meiny, to lug home my bride.

My horse was sumptuously caparisoned with scarlet stuff wrought with green, tasselled. I had my best tunic on me, of silken stuff, broidered with gold daisies, very pleasant and curious, and my cloak was of gold tissue lined with beaver. My shoes were of dressed leather, my hat was of ermine, with an eagle's feather. Afore me my pennon-bearer carried our blue pennant, with our heraldic sign, a chained lion that hath broke his chain, and the words *A deo cibum petunt.*

Now came my mother and father to the door to bless me, with Gudrun and the Mass-thane and the house-servants.

'I doubt if there bin chests enow for all the things the wench will bring,' said mother; and Gudrun said—

'Bring no witch-women, you mind!'

Then father called out.

'We bin felling the big oak for a cradle, lad, for you mind I broke the old one over that surly shepherd's poll.'

So with that I set forth.

All the way the buds peered, the birds bubbled, the leaves lapped. High May and coming on to summer it was. We sang, my men and I, digging our heels into our horses and pounding up the leavy forest roads. We shouted old songs, and monks' songs, minstrels' lays and songs of the bards. And when the light lanced green in the oak-glade where I met with Nesta first—for that way I chose to go—then we drew rein and sang in a softer chorus—

'Why were they born so beautiful?'

And every man's voice was mellow as a bird's, for every man mused upon his love. For there was no old man in the company, nor a man wed, but all were merry bachelors, lovesome and lusty and debonair.

35

All the maids at Powis were on the battlements to see us ride in, a-waving of their wimples and other gear and calling shrilly like ladies beneath the spells of wizards. There stood my love in the open door, and she was lovely as the star of eve.

In samite she was clad, so white, so soft, so shining. It did caress her here and grip her there, at hip and waist and breast, so she was utterly given to our eyne. For her mantle defended her not, sweeping out behind her, and being of ermine and Tyrian purple. The churn-owl, done in gold, clasped her mantle, and her wimple, that fell from her high peaked hat of scarlet, was sewn with small pearls.

Beside her, dressed in full armour, stood Jorwerth, even as he were the bridegroom. And it had a most discomfortable seeming to behold this one fellow all caparisoned for war when we others were in our best gowns and soft shoon. And all the evening dusky hall beyond her was full of the moth-flutterings of girls, with firelight flickering on a golden plait, a scarlet shoe, a gemmy stomacher, with a smile heady as old mead flung to this man, and a curd-white hand held out to that one, and Lady Powis giving orders unceasing and unheeded. By the fire Powis sat upon the settle, well content with a small new merlin from the Faroe Isles upon his wrist. Pleased as a lad he was, for Lady Powis would always hinder him bringing in his birds, saying they were discourteous fowl and would do that they should not afore folk.

'Powis!' cried his wife, 'here be young Polrebac. Give welcome!'

So Powis came and clapped me on shoulder, his merlin sidling and spitting like a cat.

'A pretty piece!' he said.

So I agreed it was. Then I asked Jorwerth, seeing him look like some dark devil in a mystery, why he had done on his armour. And he answered that the King's business called, and he would not abide for the marriage feast.

Then he turned and stared upon Nesta a good while, and she hung her head, as the oxeye daisy will in sweltering noon, and red overcame her alabaster and she lifted not her eyne.

Then he said 'So!'—and, suddenly stooping, put his lips to her hand, and the hall rang with her scream, and looking upon her hand I saw the scarlet blood upon its white, and the marks of teeth. Then my heart boiled, and I went after him to the horse-block, but instantly he was in the saddle and away, and the sound of his galloping and the galloping of his escort died away at last upon the quiet air.

Then did I take the Flower of the West by may-blossom hand, and stood with her afore the priest in the green-litten chapel, where upon a dark wooden rood the Christus, cunningly carven out of wood, did writhe in pain and sweat big drops most dreadful to see. So sharp the thorn, so sharp the nail! Woe's me, but I could smell the vinegar reeking upon the sponge, and the blood mingling with the heavy sweat. And the deep side-wounds, like an ancient tree-cave where children play, and the poor head, drooping, aching for his mother's breast, so greatly foredone! I shut my eyne, and so got through in some fashion, and as soon as the blessing was given I did seize Nesta by shoulder and rush for the door. And there was life and light, and a trembling of young leaves, chirping of fledglings, all the servants and riding-tenants gathered to give us joy, children and dogs, horses neighing, beggars giving blessings for alms, maidens strawing flowers, and the sumpter mules, laden with Nesta's apparel and jewels from Tochswilla, squealing and humping their hind-quarters as mules will. A musician in a scarlet cloak sat in the sun beneath the castle wall, playing upon a harp, and a big yellow-haired man like a Druid stood beside him, singing a bride song of Taliesin—'My heart awakened.' I clomb from the cave of the rood-tree, I lifted Nesta and carried her into the forest and there I set a hand on either breast, for this I had hungered to do so long, and it is great satisfaction to set one's hand on anything so round and comely, and hath in it the same pleasure as the juggler's trick, when the ball settles sweetly in its cup.

But this is carnality and must not hold us. Only strange it was how Nesta did start and tremble, as a steed will tremble if a ghost crosses his way in the forest. And because she shuddered this way and that, I took her and set her against a beech tree, and there I might set hand on breast as hard as I would and so did till she was flat against the tree, white as her gown, eyne shut and arms outspread. Then she wanned more and more, and closed her eyne fast, and the sweat stood upon her face and the tears mingled with it. Yet could I not leave moulding and crushing of her breasts for the joy and content of it. I could see the black bruises beneath the thin stuff, but cared not, laughing out in triumph. Then, as she lolled so wanly on the tree, arms out, head hanging, all dabbled in tears and sweat, it was as if the Crucified hung there. And in my rage that she should play this trick on me I smote her upon the mouth. But the moment I loosed my hold she slid down, all in a heap upon the beech-mast, and I could not wake her. So I carried her to Lady Powis, and she said—

'Why did the Almighty One make men?' Then she clouted my ears and laughed and kissed me, and doused water on Nesta and gave her a posset of herbs, so that in a while she was better, and they made her sit beside me at table, but she would not speak to me, only look sideways from her long elfin eyes in a blankness of fear, which made me pity her not at all, but only triumph, to think she could not escape me. Such wiles has Satan! So he catches our feet with wrathes of love and lust, and tumbles us in all our youthful pride.

But in a while I grew tired of sitting there with no word from Nesta, so suddenly arising I called my men out, and bade them mount, and I gave my thanks to Lord and Lady Powis for their courteous entertainment, and set my arm about Nesta and so bore her to the door and set her before me on the saddle. Then with a shout we set our horses into a gallop, pounding away in the long light of even.

But as we came into the dusk of the woods, Nesta set her hands to her mouth and gave a long, strange cry, not like the cry of any bird, nor like a herdsman's or a shepherd's, nor cries of battle or the tourney. It was most like the rising and falling of a wolf's howl, but mellower. And before ever I saw that the men crossed themselves, muttering—*Ora pro nobis*—I knew the cry for what it was, the long, mellifluous, unescapable *ululatus* of the witches. And even before she had ceased to give tongue, from deep in the forest came the answer—

'Ah lu-lule, lu-lule!'

And night seemed to fall on the instant; the night wind arose, cold and wailing from the marish lands, lifting the boughs as though it sought something there hid. Owls stirred, creatures of the night crept from covert, wolves whined beneath Breidden. The black pine-tops lifted and lapsed as in some ancient despair.

Silence had fallen on the company. No man sang nor whistled nor made coarse jests, but rode glum and grim, casting strange looks on Nesta, crossing themselves and saying what prayers they could remember. But I would not cross myself, for I feared the witches a deal less than I feared the Crucified.

★ ★ ★

Now in the life of a man there comes once a time boding Eternity—so joyous it is, so fresh and fair. Yet it is lapt in woe, like a sweet child in a caul. And as I was with Nesta in the litel grey garden I knew well that the hours were glass, bright glass, to crackle inward when God pleased.

Yet in my garden methought I had security of joy. If God ever thought of any better Paradise than dawn and June and a mountain garden, He hath not showed it to me.

It clung like a nest, this my garden, to the grey wall of our castle, and it was grey itself with the quiet greyness of doves. The lavender was all spiked over like a castle guarded by halberd-men, and the maiden pink held up fresh buds, the grey-leaved rose bloomed white beneath the heavy dews. There were no citizens of the litel grey garden save Nesta and I, the grey-brown bees and the portly grey pigeons walking in the sun, like abbots. And for me, my joy was as the joy of holy recollected folk, still, with nought in it of the raving of lust. And meseems no joy is sweeter than this. For other joys tear themselves in their raving, like seas falling upon a cliff. But this content neither stirreth nor breaketh. It is as a tree covered with hearted leaves, each in his place, none shifting, in a quiet land where no storm comes.

Within the southward wall was a niche, and there I put a bench of grey seasoned wood, and brought her there, and lay at her feet upon the warm grey stones, with the fragrance of crushed ground-ivy in my nostrils, and Nesta shining upon me in her niche of grey stone, with a white gown upon her, that it seemed like a white rose, as if her curves were the rose curves with here a fluting and there a shadow, here a shell-curl and there a silver-veined round. I had forgot, in those June days, the dark *ululatus*, the shruggings of the men, and I had forgot the urgency of the Lord.

I suppose there was never a country so quiet as ours, that is to say, quiet of men. But noised with birds it was, so that the clangour of the cuckoos was like a dinning of bells, and out of the forest the doves roared soft as paduasoy, and the hawks and eagles, wheeling high from mountain to mountain, filled the empty air with their sovereign voices. There was Balm of Gilead in my garden, and there was the pleasant comfrey and rudweed, which the French call *immortelle*. For certain hours of the day the sun played on us, basking with the bees and the green slipping lizards. And for part of the day the blue, solemn shadow of Cotardicote mountain covered it like an interdict. But Nesta bloomed in the shadow, white, rare, transparent as a shell. She spoke as birds speak. When she laughed I thought the tall lilies by the wall had given tongue. As for her thoughts, they were simple, childish and clear, like flowers you see through. Only at times, like the licking of a litel flame, would come a touch of craft, like a lizard in the crevices. Then I was ill at ease. But soon it passed and I was happy once more.

Nesta thought it would be a fine thing to have along all the walks close hedges of yew, and birds, four-legged creatures and men on horseback cut out therein, as they had in the old garden at Powis. But I told her it would be a many years afore the yew was heart-high, and a many more afore it could be cut into shapes. But she said—

'What matter? Time enow. We be young.'

'Ah, we bin young,' I answered, watching the Cotardicote shade like chicory flowers, swallowing up my garden.

'Solemn, it is,' Nesta said, 'the shadow of the big hill. When the shadow comes, the garden seems as the gardens of nunshousen, that are no gardens, but prisons. Let us come into the garden only when the shade is away.'

So we came there only with the sun, and else the garden was void, guarded by the questing bees, the abbot doves.

In the evenings, long and green, sifted with gold, while I tended the orchard, my sweet would sit in her turret-room beside the open window of horn, just as my dream had been, and she would sew at her tapestry, calling to me whiles, 'I have put in the red sword-tassel, Gilbert!' or 'I have put in the lady's mouth, sir, my love, and it is a mouth to be kissed.'

'So is thine, my soul,' I would call, throwing down the pruning knife. I ever believed in summer pruning, in especial at Polrebec, where winds were wild, and if you left your trees too heavy they would be broke in one of our thunder-storms. Then she would lean out of the narrow window, gleaming and shining like no mortal maid, with that lustrous look of porcelain, of alabaster, of Venus her shell. And suddenly rushing toward her I would lay hold of the old ivy-tree that grew upon the wall, and so climb to her. There we would sit as snug as bees in the wall and look out of our fastness and say how safe it was, even from ill-wishers, and from the witches and ghosts that came over on winter nights, darkening the air—only it was pitch-black already—for we had a great cross of wych-elm on our topmost turret, and so though they streamed over from wild lands afar, even from the Black Forest beyond the sea, yet could they not touch us.

Then, when morning came, we would go gathering wild strawberries, of which there were a many; and as summer marched onward, the wimberries ripened, purple and sweet, and we went up the mountains for them, taking each our manchet of bread and piece of cheese and our wooden bottle of milk.

'Never was such a summer!' I cried, as we raced along the green, soft, grassy Roman Way.

'But now all summers will be so,' Nesta answered.

'Dost know?' I said, and there was an urgency in my heart. 'Dost know, Nesta?'

'Ah, I know right well.'

'Why dost thou think it, my love?'

'Oh, because I am fain to think it,' she answered, laughing, and in a flash she had hidden herself in the black rocks and I could not find her.

I ran hither and thither, the sky growing dark and overcast, fearing some harm had come to her, for Satan has much power on these hills, and under shelter of storm and night he holds court there.

Then meseemed that God had taken her, so that I should turn my eyes to Himward. Yet I could not think Him so cruel. For why should He, that hath all things, begrutch to me this one creature? Yet is not the word begrutch the true word. For when our God taketh a heart and makes it void for Himself it is as the triumphal entry of the Cæsars. Which man in the throng would turn to gloat on his woman or his babes when, it may be for the one only time in his life, he beheld great Cæsar? So God coming into this life or that life fills it so plenteously that there is room for none else. And the soul, suddenly stilled, as one coming through ways barred with sunlight, hearing doves speak, seeing the heavy tree-tops tremble as beneath a footstep, murmureth—'Is it, in very truth, Thou?' And after, hour by hour, is an indwelling with Him, an ingrowing to His mighty silence.

Now all this I feared. And meseemed as I ran about the rocks that He had done this thing for a showing forth and a prophecy of what must be, soon or late. And though in a while Nesta came laughing from her covert, yet my joy was gone. And the days after were not so gay, and the secure peace of my garden was shaken.

* * *

Thus summer passed and the orchard was litten with points of scarlet, and Nesta ran here and there in her gown of scarlet trimmed with swan feathers, gathering the fruit with baskets of rushes. And soon all was stored in the upper room of the turret, and we had salted our meat and smoked it, and all was winter-safe. In the forest the leaves fell, turning in the air as the trencher does in the game, with a weariness and a despair in their twirling, as if to say, 'What matter where we go?—since we be already as good as dead.' Mist stood horse-high there all day, and afore evening the wolves began their restless whining. From dawn to sunset the covert and gallop past our moat, as if some panic thought possessed them, and in the fitful moonlight the owls voiced some old despair. Now at the time of sloe-gathering, my aunt Gudrun was busy making cordial and grumbling that no visitors came our way. For in great places like Powis there was always a stir of coming and going—a gleeman with some new lay in praise of the lord of the place, or men-at-arms lost in the uncharted forest, or a distressed lady whose paramour had been slain and her pavilion burnt to the ground, she herself escaping only through the speed of her jennet and her swiftness in departing while the marauders had their thoughts on other matters. And to those great places there would often come trains of sumpter mules, their owners asking for hospitality, or an abbot or a cardinal passing by in state, or even the King himself, sending an outrider afore him to order stately preparations, and heralded by trumpets. But as Gudrun said, in so small a castle, hid away between mountain and woodland in the great silence of those places, far alike from the broader riding-ways in the woods and the mule-tracks over the hills, what visitors could be looked for between the fall of the leaf and May day?—saving maybe a starveling hermit, frozen out of his anchorage and desiring sustenance at the season of Christmas.

Now it was our custom, so soon as the autumn night drew in, wild and wet and stark and stormy, to gather about the hearth and cheer ourselves with remembered songs and old tales, while the ladies spun the fleeces of summer wool or stooped to their embroidering. I would whittle elder pipes and whistles for my dogs or hollow out cups from lumps of wood, or fashion arrows. The storm would shake our door, the wolves would snuff at our threshold, the witches would go screaming overhead up on the snow-clouds; and at curfew we, having said our Paternosters, lay down in peace and

41

content. And yet, in truth, we did not measure the deepness of our peace until it was shattered like a bowl of fine glass.

It was a night of deep stifling fog, that rose from the marishes like a cerement and wrapped us away from life. We sat in the red firelight, and Nesta sang snatches of curious songs and gipsy lays, and she said she was glad she was not of those folk that in summer she would lief follow, but now she was very glad to be so safe, as the burrowing mole and the waxen-sealed bee, with warmship and food till the sweet May weather came again.

'Safe from all harm!' she cried.

'Aye, by Goddes mercy,' said my mother, pale, as if she felt some portent drawing nigh, and she crossed herself.

And suddenly, in the deep silence, there came a thundering upon the door, so that we looked at one another aghast, and my mother said—

'It is the Elf King. Open not!'

But a voice cried upon us to open for the love of heaven, and on the silent air shuddered the voices of the wolf-pack.

Nesta, hearing a single human voice without, cried, 'Maybe it is some great lord in golden armour,' and ran to open. There was the great white empty square of night; but no great knight in golden armour.

Nesta peered out, and then, turning with a shriek, rushed past me as I went to the doorway.

'What is it, child?' asked my mother. 'What has affrighted thee? Who is there, calling from the dark?'

'Go not to the door, Gilbert,' cried Nesta. 'Go not. It is some strange one—something evil and fearsome. I know not—Oh, shut the door, Gilbert! Shut it out, into the night where it belongeth.'

Even as I went across the hall I said in my heart—'She had lief it had been Jorwerth,' and a sudden grief struck across my peace, and it was as it is after a night of rain in May—the orchard saddened, the blossom fallen, the fair promise of fruit broken and forsworn. The grey, throttling fog stood up before the door, the forest was silent. This was a great marvel, for it never was so but in fog. In all other weathers it sang and whispered, but mostly it roared and shouted, so that when I rode there with Nesta in these days of autumn I must yell my little lovewords as if I were shouting my men on to battle. But on this night it was struck mute as with great horror, and a pine cone falling made a great startling noise. In the dumb woods only the whining of the wolves, a thin cold sound, flickered here and there like licking flames.

Then, looking down, I saw what had affrighted Nesta. For there, all across the threshold, lay the half naked body of a man—though you had easier said a log of gnarled wood. So twisted and lean and brown, with his ribs standing out, and his hair long and wild as pine boughs—I thought may be it was some strange thing out of the trees—a satyr or tree-soul or some kind of pixie. So I made the sign of the cross afore I stooped to lift it from where it lay. My father was come to the door by this time, and between us we lifted in the gaunt fearsome creature, naked but for its piece of wolf-skin. Even as we pulled him in and made fast the door, there came a sudden keen skirling round the corner of the keep, and the vanguard of the wolf-pack flung themselves against the door.

'Well, brother?' said my father. But the man lay for dead, and Gudrun took him as it were for her own prey.

'Go all of ye,' she cried, 'and leave me fettle the poor soul. Fetch you me my leeches, Gilbert.'

'There seemeth not blood in him enough for a new-born leech,' said my father. 'I fear me the poor soul has ill-wishers—even as I—even as I.'

'Thine have not made thee lean,' said Gudrun. 'I am sure I would lief they did so. It would save a mort of leechings and sweatings.'

'But this man,' said mother, 'is of a lean habit even from his cradle. And also he hath a monkish look. Maybe he is some poor brother that hath sinned and is fleeing from the wrath of his abbot. If that is so,'—she looked at father, quiet and yet firm,—'if that is so, we will give him refuge.'

'What, woman? What, my dear? You'd bring the Church upon my back, as if I had not ill-wishers enow? Eh, eh, why did God make Eve? 'Twas a thought should have been nipped, like a frosted rose. But there He was, so soon as He thought of it, dreaming on it like a gleeman on some new ditty, thinking here and thinking there, putting in a whimsey in one place and a shriek in another place, like one needling at the tapestry, leaving Adam to be led into mischief and get on as best he could, whereas'—my father pointed his finger at the stranger stretched deathly upon the hearth, as if he were preaching at him—'whereas He might have made something of Adam.'

'Thou speakest without reverence, my dear,' mother said. 'Come then, let us go to our chamber and pray awhile for this poor soul. He hath a far-away look, as if he came from foreign lands. As if—she went on, speaking dreamy as a dove, as she ever did when the prophet's mood came to her—'as if he came with tidings—dark tidings—a word like a sword to cut love to the bone. Ah! Ah! not that, O Lord! Not that!' She covered her face as one in agony. Then with a look I never saw on her face afore, a look of guile, even of craft, she turned to my father, saying—

'He is dead, my dear. If we keep him, we can only say Mass for him and bury him—we cannot bring him to life. And if the pursuers find him here, maybe there will be trouble for us all. Let us then,' she murmured, her face white as new parchment, 'let us open the door a little and put him where he was. The wolves—they will leave no trace—'

Her voice trailed away, lost like a candle flame in the wind.

My father stared at her as one might gaze on Our Lady if she spoke as a harlot.

'What? What? Thou that art all mercy, to will and wish that I throw a guest to the wolves? What ails thee?'

'He is dead,' said mother, sullen.

'Nay,' said Gudrun, busy about him. 'He breathes, and hath swallowed some mead. I shall bring him back to life.'

'Busybody and fool!' cried mother, and gathering up her gown, she ran across the room and smote Gudrun on the cheek.

'She is mad,' said father. 'The sight of a stranger hath turned her brain.'

And indeed it seemed as if she were mad. She snatched the leeches from me and flung them into the fire. She took the cup of mead from Gudrun and flung that after them.

But Gudrun cared not, for simples and cures were to her what his picture is to a painter, and she fetched more mead and lifted the man up that he might the easier swallow it. As she did so, an emblem, tied within the wolf-skin by a thong of leather, slipped out. Gudrun cried—

'Why see, it is the Crusaders' emblem, that of which they have told us—the emblem Peter Hermit gives to his followers.'

It was like a piece of whitish money, and on it a cross in red-scarlet.

It lay there on the rushes twixt my mother and Gudrun, and seeing it my mother seemed possessed. She ran to the trestle-table, where supper yet stood, and snatching up the great knife wherewith my father hacked the meat, she rushed upon the man, uplifting the knife in both hands, as if in some rite of the Druids long ago, and she would have brought it down into the poor fellow's heart, but Gudrun, with the mothering love that is somewhere in many healers, did defend him. So she and my mother wrestled for it, and my father and I gaped upon the scene, the like of which had never afore been in our quiet house.

I looked towards Nesta to see if she was afeard, and once more I was astonished. For Nesta, that was so timid most times, was doubled up with laughter, and of a truth there was something of oddity in it, that these two ladies of stately bearing and ripe age should so punch and clout one another like foolish mommets in the showman's hand. But it seemed strange to me that Nesta, who was in all respects like Our Lady to look upon, should laugh so unseemly when an innocent man and a helpless was in danger of his life. By this, the dogs, fiercened by the uproar and by the smell of the blood that was pouring from Gudrun's big fleshy nose—for my mother had given her some shrewd blows—were snarling and growling about the swooning man, and my father and I must beat them off with our staves. That done, my father seized hold of mother, and afore she had time to struggle, rushed with her to her chamber, set her within and bolted the door; then returning, wiping his face with the sleeve of his jerkin, he said—

'Well now? Well now? What more is to do?'

Gudrun was tending the man again, satisfied. In a little while he stirred and opened black eyes like caverns, looking darkly and wildly upon us as one that had no map of the country of our souls, dwelling in sterner places. He sat up, dazed, and Gudrun fed him with warm mead and afterward with meat and bread. My father fetched his cloak and folded it about him. And all the while my mother beat upon her door, crying aloud, and the wolves scurried about the castle and about, howling.

Nesta had given over laughing now that the fighting was done. She was ever one to see the oddity of an action, but not of a thought, and to see the horror of a violent death, but not of a hid, soul-killing grief.

* * *

And, writing all these things now, not only she but all of us, then, seem unreal as wanton fays in dreamy, moony worlds.

For now, what ails me? Am I not housed in Goddes hand? Looking backward, I find nought in those stirring days like the guerdon of my present peace. I go out into the clear blue air, when God His sun shines hot and golden; and, resting upon the cliff, level with the top of a fruited sycamore, I look down through the lipping green to the lipping blue and watch the long quiet waves come in through the crevices of the leavy boughs. And after a while, turning and looking upward at the rocky steep behind me, I see, on the cliff top, the yellow-gold of toadflax blazing against the porcelain heavens. And what with so much light and so much warmship, the world bedecked with banners, doves crooning, seas murmuring, stars in silver armour waiting beyond the blue to sentinel the night and God indwelling, it is as if, escaping the *rigor mortis*, I had come to heaven by the little path made for children, and so was already in beatitude. For now the pain that was so sharp is done, and the hands that clung to me, the voices that called to me, He hath gathered to Himself, and they that lured me frommet now persuade me toerts His glory, whither I pray it may please Him to bring all men.

But on the evening of which I am telling there was nothing of peace, but only heartbreak and bepuzzlement of the soul. I looked about my familiar home where the early sun was used to slant in through the arrow-slits, barring the floor with gold, and all day the sweet-scented rushes, that my mother would have new-gathered every morning, made the hall fresh and pleasant, and in the evening the westering sun stole in once more, from the opposite arrow-slits, and later the moon came with silver bars for gold. And all so ordered and so peaceful, the great coffers of meal around the walls, the drinking-horns and wooden cups and trenchers all decently set upon a shelf of oak, my mother's tapestry-work by the largest loophole with her spinning-wheel, our hunting-horns and armour on the wall, and the flickering lights from the ever-burning fire of logs shining on silver helmets and drawing a hundred gleams from the bright chain-mail. From the beams hung smoked salmon and other fish and dried haunches of venison and flitches of wild boar. There, too, hung my mother's herbs— thyme, sweet basil, marjoram and rue, rosemary, fennel and wild spikenard. There also were Gudrun's simples. In a deep nook beyond the hearth stood wooden vats of honey, well covered, and casks of mead and a few flagons of rare red wine given to my father long ago by the Conqueror when he came here, surveying for Doomsday Book, a little while after my mother and father were wed. There was the settle and beside it my father's tall carven chair. Just where the eastern sunrays touched it, hung upon the wall a cross of oak, with Christ upon it, but not, as it were, in pain, only drooping, as a lily at midsummer, seeming to sleep. Outside upon the roof the pigeons crooned and the bell rang drowsily for matins and prime and evensong. It seemed a place whose peace only the last trumpet, pealing from the tower of heaven, could break. Even the dogs were quiet in their minds, resting chin on paws with one eye shut, not brawling among themselves. Our serving men and maids were sober and honest, the wenches not levering overmuch, good with their spindles, knowing how to cleanse and full the wearing apparel in the shallow stony brook that goes across the way from below our hill up to the hill of Cotardicote. Nor would they drink the milk from the wooden buckets when they went milking in the meadow, nor listen to pixies, nor put their fingers in the honey-vats. But they would cluster together by the door when my father prayed of an evening, as frighted sheep will gather, and when he said the *Ora pro nobis* they would answer all together—

'And also for us, poor souls.'

* * *

On a summer afternoon, about milking time, you could not find a pleasanter place than this our hall, with the door opened wide on the rolling woods, the sunlight streaming in, the air, full of the fragrancy of aromatic leaves, blossoms and the flower of the grass, coming in heady and full of life. There was the cauldron simmering above the logs, and there were the cattle lowing in the beeves' field, and in the forest, near and far, the sweet roaring of the doves. If any folk came, they felt the peace of it and slipped into the life of the place and troubled it not at all. But this being, who lay now before the hearth, was other. The safety of the place seemed to shrink and wither before him. It seemed that the comfort we set store by and the sorrows we feared were all alike to him. For a man who has battled through a torrent heeds not the rain beating in at the loopholes, and a man who has been a long while tortured does not complain of a toothache. He seemed to be under governance of his own law and none other's, and he seemed of very sad cheer and also without pity. As he lay there, brown as wood, it seemed to me as if the wooden Christus had come down from the wall and was now tended by Gudrun, whispering to us with pale lips, staring upon us with cavernous eyes.

It was late, near to midnight, when at last he came quite to himself and stood afore the hearth, gaunt and of great stature, seeming to carry upon his back a shadowy Cross. And ever as I gazed on him, meseemed he was made not of flesh and blood but of hollow wood. His caverns of eyne were hollow, and his voice as he now uplifted it was hollow also, and rolled around the silent place like lost winds blowing from the crypts of empty night where yet God has created nothing. There was, as it were, no yea in him. His word was a nay-word. His rule was denial. He dwelt in shadow.

He lifted up his lean, long arm, and the cresset flaring behind him set its gnarled shadow on the other wall.

He set his devouring eyes upon me.

'Young man,' he said, 'I say unto thee, arise and come. The Lord hath need of thee.'

At these words there came a shriek from where my mother was, so sharp it seemed it must have cut her heart in two.

We stared upon the man.

'Gilbert Polrebec,' he said, in his strange tongue, mingled of Saxon and some country French, 'I come from Peter Hermit. Thou must return with me now, swiftly, for because of his old kindness for thy mother he wills that thou go with him in this first glorious Crusade, walking beside him as his own familiar friend. Multitudes that none can number will be about thee, marching Godward, and if thou diest there will be a seat for thee in the innermost circle of the heavens at God His elbow.'

'Cruel and evil one!' shrieked Nesta, and rushing at the man she smote him on the face with a litten torch.

I put my arms about her to restrain her. But it seemed the man cared no more for blazing torches than for wolves. He went on speaking, calm as a Mass-thane in his own chapel, though the hot pine-resin had seared his cheek all across.

My father meanwhile sat down heavily in his chair, as if his knees would not uphold him.

'If thou wilt not leave father and mother and wife, housen and lands, thou art not worthy of me, saith the Lord.'

My father spoke, and his voice was hoarse and shaken as an old man's voice.

'The lad is but young, sir.'

'We desire the young,' the man replied.

'And lately wed.'

'In heaven is no marrying nor giving in marriage.'

'And we be aging folk, his mother and my own self, and we have ill-wishers and we need our son.'

'The Lord hath ill-wishers also, in all the towns of Galilee, and He commandeth Gilbert Polrebec to fight in His behalf.'

Now, seeing him stand afore the image of our Lord, it seemed that my thoughts grew moithered, so I could not tell which was the stranger and which was Christus, or whether Christus had been in peril of wolves and recovered by Gudrun, or whether the one that summoned, speaking with so stern voice, summoned in truth from the comfortless tree that hung upon the wall.

'Would to God,' cried my father, 'that we had a Mass-thane here, or somebody to advise us. The ways of God be past finding out, and indeed it seemeth at times as if He was our chief ill-wisher.'

His mouth was trembling like a fretful babe's.

'Speak not blasphemy,' said the intruder.

'There be plenty of lusty lads at Stretton-in-the-Dale,' said Gudrun. 'Lads with too much of Satan in them, that Jerusalem might cure. Many's the house with half a score of them. Go there, good sir, and call some of these and leave this lad, that is the prop and stay of the house.'

'Did that Blessed One, on the bitter Cross, have prop and stay? Is a man better than his Master?'

Then he uplifted his loud, cold voice, ah! cold as the winter wind on the heights of Stiperstones, and it rolled and echoed about the room above the roaring of the fire and the howling of the wolves and my mother's urgent beating on the door that had begun again.

'Young man! I say unto thee, arise! A crown of glory and a trophy of stars, dominion in Paradise and the thanks of God His Mother—or, if thou refuse, anathema maranatha!'

Then he set his eyes upon me, sucking out my soul, and as I looked into his eyes it seemed to me that he had looked on all the world and found it waste and wilderness.

So, turning anywhere to save me from his eyes, that caught me and lured me into a spell of terror, I looked toward the Christus on the wall. And behold, a dreadful marvel! For even as I looked, the image shuddered and two tears rolled down the face, and He did bat His eyes at me. And when I saw the Lord God so shuddering and weeping upon our wall, and when, in the manner of some poor babe denied of some sweetmeat or some revel, He did so bat His eyes and droop His head, I knew that I must go, and my heart turned in my side and my soul uttered a cry, and I forgot myself, falling on darkness.

And so in the grey dawn we departed, leaving the castle all blinded and folded in mist, and the litel grey garden blotted out, and those three beloved ones weeping and groaning at the door where I was to go in and out no more until many a year was fled. But in the wan light of morning I saw that the Christus on the rood wept no more, nor batted His eyes, but seemed more at ease, satisfied as a child at some promise long withheld but at last given.

* * * * *

Now I might tell you from this hour onward of journeyings and wanderings, strange folk, wild lands, fightings, processions with banners, horrid sights by land and sea, of endless roads, of multitudes that none could number, the mingled colours of their garments rolling like a river, resistless, eastward; of old folk fainting, left by the way to die; of little children, barefoot, singing in fluty voices, trudging barefoot in the white dust. For Peter ever had at heart the thought of a children's crusade, which blessed thought, though he never saw it come into fruition, may yet be brought about, and will be so great a portent, so strange a sight, that the Turks might well forget their arms, falling into an amazement under the spell of innocence. And doubtless in God's own time this miracle will come to pass, and the world will see childhood like a banner streaming across the world in colours of apple-blow and gold, led on by one riding a white foal, not seen, but known to be there ever in the van, a grave-eyed lad with wonder in his gaze, in favour with God and man, with kindly bearing and a winning smile—the Carpenter's Son.

But I cared nothing at all for these high matters as I started out with my harsh companion in that dawn that seemed as night, and saw the white fog take my beloved ones, and saw my little castle, my refuge against the sorrows of the world, suddenly engulfed, as a beaver's house when the bore cometh up Severn. Our comfortless journeying, our perils and oft-threatened death, what cared I for them? God had stretched His hand for me, as the chess-player for a pawn. I was without will or wish. There, in that sweet peace of other days, so near, but gone, was my Nesta's golden head, haloed ever to my sight, and my mother's grave and gentle glance, my father's rough kindness. All, even Gudrun, stood in the rose-light of heaven. And I could not reach them—I was a dumb beast driven hither and thither.

Only one blessing was mine, above that of other Crusaders. Namely, that being in attendance on Peter himself, my whereabouts were known, and three times during the seven years I was away I had news from Polrebec. This was great mercy of God, and I think saved me from madness.

It was in the third summer of my journeying that the first letter came, sent by my dear mother. It seemed that a learned friar from Lilleshall, having come to ask a night's lodging on his way to Bishop's Castle on business of the monastery, had spoken of his writing, how he was making a fair missal to the glory of God. So my mother made bold to tell of her longing to send some word of home to me, that was her only son and had been with Peter Hermit three winters—which was a long while for a mother's heart, though she knew well he was safe in keeping of our dear Lord, but was feared he would miss to have his clean linen and his posset of herbs, spring and autumn, as Gudrun prepared for all at Polrebec; and she was feared of his hastiness in some brawl, and of the long roads wearying his poor feet, that were inclined to be flat even from a boy.

So the friar tarried two more nights, and wrote the letter in good Latin.

I mind we were at the township of Siena when the letter came to me. Peter was preaching there, and we had a high chamber in a monastery where I could hear through the unglazed window the sound of the copper-workers' hammers, making bowls and cups, and could see, when rain threatened, the blue mountains come nigh and take on the colour of hyacinthus, so that it seemed to me I looked upon Cotardicote and heard again our smith working at his anvil in the stithy under the hill. And when bells sounded and the cypresses rustled in the night wind, I could well believe that I heard the bell within Nesta's turret, and our yew-tree, that was already a small tree when Christ died, harping to its own soul as it stood beside the drawbridge. I was musing on them all at home, how Gudrun would be gathering her simples and father busy at the sheep-washing, and Nesta maybe carding wool in the grey garden with the lavender coining into blow, and mother pacing the turret whence could be seen a piece of the bare road beyond Werentenhale. Here I knew she would go every day, hoping that she might see on the ell of white road a rider whom she would know on the instant, though man and horse seem at that distance elfin-small.

So, as I was thinking all these things, Peter himself came in, his arms flailing, as ever when he was stirred, and his black eyes blazing.

He said—

'Gilbert, set out the wooden bowls and platters—and go to the wine-shop for a flagon of red wine, and buy bread and meat, honeycomb, melons and fish—for, behold! Wolfran, whom I sent to England to gather souls, is at the city gate with a large following of pilgrims. Wolfran is an ancient friend to me, and I would fain entertain him and those with him in the best manner.'

I was astonished at the largeness of his orders, for (as I knew to my cost) a crust and a sup of water was, to his mind, enough for a man to do a day's marching on. But to gather in so many more souls when we were even now about to set forth again was the greatest good that could befall him, and much to the glory of God; so it was no harm for that time to entertain these folks in good fashion. And I must confess that even at this distance of time I can remember that day as a red letter day; for, as well as my letter, I got such a great meal as I had not known since I left Salopia. I was then only in my 'prentice days, so not used to fasting, and it irked me sorely.

What with broiling the fish and serving the guests with them, it was late and full moonlight afore I could read my letter which this Wolfran who led the pilgrims hither had brought to me.

For the friar who wrote the letter sent it to a religious house in London Town, and they, knowing of Wolfran's company, entrusted it to him.

There was a silver flood of moonlight on the floor of our chamber, and the lisping of the cypresses filled the night, as I broke the seal and spread the parchment on the table. It was writ in good Latin, and it was curious to my mind to think of my mother's words coming to me in this tongue which she never knew even so much as a word of. And it was strange also to feel the mind of the priest in the letter, mingled with my mother's. I could not understand all the words, but must wait till morning and ask a learned priest who lived near by. Yet I made out the sense of the letter and some-whiles could well nigh hear my mother's gentle voice calling across the bushes of rue and the bushes of balm—'Gilbert! Gilbert! Thy supper waits.'

Now this is the letter in little, done into Saxon as I write. For I have it still, yellow and worn, and also the two others.

To the Glory of God and His Mother this letter is wrote to my son now in the army of the Lord marching to Hierusalem.

'I write to tell thee, Gilbert, that all are well here, and thy father hale, but he works later than is right and should have a radman in your place. Nesta grows more beautiful but more cold toward us, I cannot tell why. She hath been away to Tochswilla two times, she vanishes away afore dawn and returns in her own good time. Gudrun says there is some necromancy in it and that when she returns there is a still green light about her and a taint of wizardry. But I know not, she seemeth a simple enough creature, loving to sing and dance and play ball in the court and go hawking when thy father can awhile to take her.

'She hath brought back some more rich gauds from Tochswilla, and a little yellow witchwoman to be her tiring-maid. She is most strange, and I am feared of her. I would thou hadst not gone, my son, for indeed there be many loutish ones about might well have been spared. Yet can we not judge whom God would have, and all must be as He wills, and this we must ever have in mind—

"Quia amore langueo".'

This piece, as I could tell, was put in by the friar.

The country hath been much disturbed with brawlings and disputes caused by the decrees of Jorwerth and his escheating many folk of their estates for some fault he found. He hath been here two times and stayed a good while. I had ado to give him the fare he is used to have, and we killed all the ducks and capons and some oxen and sheep we could ill spare, for he brought a great following, that sate in the guard-room and sang songs that were not for the ears of good women. Nesta was fain of all the noise and busyness, and she would sit by the door to see them go to and fro, and she would take the Roman goblet for my lord to drink from when he stopped by the drawbridge to call out a greeting. This angered me, for as you know, Gilbert, I am so choice of it, I would scarce use it even for your caudle-cup, and other treasures and relics of our family did she fetch out for this man's pleasure, so that they were in danger of destruction. Yet must we call to mind that our dear Lord said, "Set not your affections on things below, where moth and rust corrupt."

'*Ora pro nobis.*

'Yet should not a daughter-law behave discourteous to the relics and treasures of the family into which she hath come.' ...

OVER THE HILLS AND FAR AWAY

MARGARET MAHUNTLETH, in the corner of the big settle, basked in the hearth-glow like one newly come to heaven. Warm light reddened her knitted shawl, her white apron, and her face, worn and frail. It was as if the mortal part of it had been beaten thin by the rains and snows of long roads, baked, like fine enamel, by many suns, so that it had a concave look—as though hollowed out of mother o' pearl. Some faces gather wrinkles with the years, like seamed rocks on mountains, others only become, like stones in a brook, smoother, though frailer, in the conflicting currents. Margaret's was one of these. And though she was a bit of a has-been, yet her face, as it shone from the dark settle-back, seemed young and almost angelic in its irrefragable happiness. For Marg'ret had never dreamed (no, not for an instant!) as she fought her way to Thresholds Farm through weather that made her whole being seem a hollow shell, that she would be invited into the kitchen. Usually she did her work in the barn. For Marg'ret was a chair-mender.

She travelled, on her small birdlike feet, all over the county, carrying her long bundle of rushes. With these she mended chairs at farms and cottages and even in the kitchens of rectories and in parish rooms and at the backs of churches where the people from the almshouses sat. She mended chairs mostly for other people to draw up to glowing fires and well-spread tables. She made them very flawless for weddings. For funerals she made them strong, because the people who attend funerals are generally older than those who attend weddings, and the weight of years is on them, and they have gathered to themselves, like the caddis worm, a mass of extraneous substance.

For dances Marg'ret also made them strong, knowing that in the intervals young women of some twelve stone would subside upon the knees of stalwarts rising fifteen stone.

Marg'ret knew all about it. She had been to some of the dances years ago, but people forgot to ask her to dance. Her faint tints, her soft, sad, downcast eye, her sober dress, all combined with her personality to make her fade into any background. She was always conscious, too, of the disgrace of being only a chair-mender; of not being the gardener's daughter at the Hall, or Rectory-Lucy. So people forgot she was there, and she even forgot she was there herself.

She worked hard. She could make butter-baskets and poultry-baskets through which not the most centrifugal half-dozen fowls could do more than insinuate anxious heads. She could make children's ornamental basket-chairs, and she could do the close wicker-work of rocking-chairs for nursing-mothers. Winter and summer she tramped from place to place, over frozen roads and dusty roads and all the other kinds of roads, calling at farms with her timid knock and her faint cry, plaintive and musical, soon lost on the wind—'Chairs to mend!'

Then she would take the chair or basket or mat into the orchard or the barn, and sit at her work through the long green day or the short grey day, plaiting with her pale, hollow hands. Within doors she never thought of going. She would have been the first to deprecate sheeding rushes all o'er. The warm kitchen was a Paradise to which she, a Peri, did not pretend. Its furnishings she knew intimately, but she knew them as a church-cleaner might know the altar and its chalices, being, if such a thing were possible, excommunicated. Under the bowl of the sky, across the valleys she came, did her work featly as an elf, and was gone, as if the swift airs had blown her away with the curled may-petals of spring, the curved leaves of autumn.

If night drew on before she had done her work, she would sleep in the hayloft. Nobody inquired where she usually slept, any more than they concerned themselves about the squirrel that ran along the fence and was away, or the thistledown that floated along the blue sky.

So Marg'ret had never dreamed of being invited to the hearth-place. It was the most wonderful thing. Outside, the wan snowflakes battered themselves upon the panes like birds, dying. The night had come, black, inevitable, long. And to those who have no house the night is a wild beast. In every chimney a hollow wind spoke its uncontent. There were many chimneys at Thresholds Farm. It was a great place, and the master was a man well-thought-of, rich.

Marg'ret trembled to think she was here in the same room with him. He might even speak to her. He sat on the other side of the hearth while the servant-girl laid tea—the knife-and-fork tea of farms, with beef and bacon and potatoes. A tea to remember.

He sat leaning forward, his broad, knotted hands on his knees, staring into the fire. The girl slammed the teapot down on the table and said,

'Yer tea, master.'

Marg'ret got up. She supposed it was time now for her to creep to bed in the hospitable loft, after a kindly cup of tea in the back kitchen. It had been wonderful, sitting here— just sitting quietly enjoying the rest and the dignity of the solid furniture and the bright fingers of the firelight touching here a willow-pattern plate and there a piece of copper. It was one of those marvellous half-hours of a life-time, which blossom on even to the grave, and maybe afterwards. She had never dreamed—

She softly crept towards the door, but as she went the master lifted his gloomy chestnut-coloured eyes under their thatch of grizzled hair, and so transfixed her. She could not move with that brown fire upon her, engulfing her. So he always looked when he was deeply stirred. So he had looked down at his father's coffin long ago, at his mother's last year. So he had looked into the eyes of his favourite dog, dying in his arms. The look was the realization of the infinite within the finite, altering all values. Never once in all fifteen years during which she had been calling here, had he seemed to look at Marg'ret at all.

In the almost ferocious intensity of the look she felt faint. Her face seemed like a fragile cup made to hold an unexpressed passion which was within his soul, which must find room for itself somewhere, as the great bore of water that rushes up a river must find room, some valley, some dimple where it may rest, where it may spread its strangled magnificence. She stood. Firelight filled her hollow palms; her apron, gathered in nervous fingers, so that it looked like a gleaner's, ready to carry grain; the pale shell of her face.

The servant-girl, perturbed by some gathering emotion that had come upon the kitchen, remained with a hand on the teapot-handle, transfixed. Marg'ret trembled, saying no word. How shall a conch-shell make music unless one lends it a voice? She was of the many human beings that wait on the shores of life for the voice which so often never comes.

Suddenly the master of the house said loudly, with his eyes still hard upon her—

'Bide!'

It was as if the word burst a dam within him.

Her being received it.

'Bide the night over,' he added, in the same strange thunderous voice.

She took that also into her soul.

'And all the nights,' he finished, and a great calm fell upon him. It had taken all the years of his life till now for the flood to find its valley.

Then seeing that she stood as mute and still as ever, he said—

'Coom then, take bite and sup.'

And when she was seated, like a half-thawed winter dormouse at its first feast, he said to the servant-girl, who still remained holding the Britannia-metal teapot (which seemed to mock Marg'ret with its inordinate convexity)—

'Make a bed for the Missus!'

He was determined that no misunderstanding should vex his new-found peace, and when the girl had gone, breathing hard like an exhausted swimmer, he remained staring at Marg'ret in a kind of hunger for giving. And she, perfectly receptive, empty-handed as a Peri, let his flaming eyes dwell on her face, let his fire and his food hearten her, and so gave him her charity. And this was how Marg'ret Mahuntleth, the poor chair-mender, without will of her own or desert of her own, as far as she could see, came to be the mistress of the house and lawful wife of the master of Thresholds.

THE PRIZE

I

THE vicarage lawn, bright green in the August sunshine, with beds of golden violas, had been galvanized into frantic gaiety by the incursion of the entire village. It was the great day of the year in Cherrington Magna; for the school treat and the festival of the local club had been rolled into one enormous revel. A tea, a dance, and races were included in the programme. Tea was over and, with the lusty country scorn of digestion which prevails at such festivals, everybody was now prepared to run races. Their faces shone with pleasure, hope of useful prizes, and honest yellow soap. They were of the good but unemotional type produced by preoccupation with the material side of life, and they had the touch of harshness which comes from absorption in petty worries. The women's dresses, of homely stuffs, in neutral or primary colours, made dark or brilliant patches on the green grass.

Apart from the rest, in deepest black, stood a tall, rather harsh-featured woman, who seemed to have about her something of the atmosphere of the pariah. She leaned against the churchyard wall in the purple shadow of the yew-tree, which spread its flat, dark masses over the daisied lawn from the dank enclosure of the churchyard, and she had the look of a creature at bay—sullen, and inexpressive. She was of the age that corresponds to the apple-tree's time of hard, green fruit, half-way between maturity and middle age. She had the spare angularity and weathered complexion of all field-workers. Yet, although she had no beauty, she was, in a curious subtle way, arresting. She had the air of remoteness that some people always take with them, so that their lives seem to move to a different rhythm from the lives around them, and one surprises in their eyes an impassioned secrecy, and feels in their presence the magnetism of great things for ever unrevealed. She stood fronting a little crowd.

'I'll run for pig,' she said.

'What?' cried Mrs. Parton of the shop, roundly, 'd'you mean to tell me, Selina Stone, as you're going to run for pig, and your lawful 'usband lying by lonesome over the churchyard wall?'

A slight flicker of emotion lit Selina's face and passed. It might have been anger or scorn or even mirth.

'I'll run for pig,' she repeated tonelessly.

The sexton's wife took up the argument as of inalienable right. 'And poor Bobbie Stone only measured for coffin Friday was a week!'

'Scarce cold! Scarce cold!'

59

This was from Mrs. Marsh, the washerwoman, whose face was large and white, and had the appearance of perpetually reflecting the full moon, and whose hands were always bleached and wrinkled and water-logged. But her feet were, as she put it, 'as the Lord made 'em,' and she intended to compete for the pig, and would have been pleased to know that Selina, with her long tireless legs, was out of it.

'It's not what the Vicar will like,' said Miss Milling, the schoolmistress, very quiet in grey silk, and having the air of politely ignoring the world, the flesh, and the devil.

Jane, the Vicar's cook, whose hair was so tidy that it looked like black paint, said 'That it inna!' She was going to run herself, as proxy for her sister, whose complaint it was that Providence, while giving her an enormous progeny and thus making her both need and deserve bacon at Christmas, saw fit every year to incapacitate her for competing for the pig by decreeing that she should be in the family way. So Jane was to run for the family, and she felt that she was supremely in the right, and that this muscular Selina had no call to triumph over her slight stoutness (due to the generous living at the vicarage) by thus breaking all the laws of good taste.

Jane's sister looked up from suckling the latest addition to the family. 'She's got no little uns to feed. She dunna need bacon,' she said decisively.

A murmur that matched the wind in the yew tree ran over the group, a shocked, and withal an interested, sigh.

'Run she will!'

'Dear 'eart, to think of it!'

'Run for pig, and poor Bob not sodded!'

'You're a bad 'oman, Selina Stone!'

Selina's sallow face looked sallower. She swallowed hard, but she gazed unflinchingly into the moon-face of the washerwoman, and she remained self-poised, like a heavy pebble in a water-course. She held on to her own personality, though whelmed in the currents of public opinion.

Jane's sister tried the human note, looking up over the bundle that was her new, creased, enthralling baby.

'My dear, you've no need to do any such thing. Bob was insured, as I very well know. Think how my little uns could enjoy that dear little pig come Christmas. Dunna rob them! Of such is the kingdom of 'eaven.'

'Amen!' said her husband.

Three or four girls looked at their young men and giggled. Save for these young men, the race would have been a walk-over for them, but the consciousness of admiring eyes seriously disturbed their breathing and, by the justice of things, gave the older folk a chance.

'Selina! O Selina Stone!' quavered a very old man with an impressive falsetto voice. 'You'll ne'er run, my wench?'

'Ah, I'll run.'

'You'll fall afore the fall of the leaf if you do wrong by the dead.'

'Oot give it up if Vicar says no?'

Selina, weary of repetition, merely shook her head and leaned back against the churchyard wall. Hostile eyes focused themselves upon her, hostile thoughts washed over her. A man pushed his way through the little crowd and came to her.

'My girl,' he said, stooping so that she could hear his undertone, 'best not! Looks queer-like. Ye can have a plenty of bacon when ye set up with me.'

People nudged each other. This was Bill Jakeways, the hedger, to whom, it was said, Selina had given all he asked when, in sultry summer evenings, she had worked overtime, hoeing turnips, and he had done piecework at the hedges between hay-harvest and corn-harvest. What he had ever seen in her had always been a puzzle to the village. He might have taken his pick, it was said. He was the best-looking man in the place, a splendid creature, like a statue, minded like the naïve dumb things of wood and meadow. Like a dumb creature he had worked for Selina, carrying water, lugging wood, helping her in the fields.

'I won'er what Stone thinks of it!'

This was one of the village phrases. But Bobbie Stone, slight and frail and tired, coughing now and again over his bespoke boots in Selina's tidy kitchen, had never divulged by any word or look what he thought. He and Selina had lived like middle-aged people, far outside the scope of passion. He would look up and smile when she came in from the fields to get his tea of bacon and potatoes; and if she was late and more flushed than usual he never seemed to notice it. They were judged by the village to be well matched, for she had always been poor favoured and he was not much of a chap—a rickety piece.

So life went on until Bobbie, coughing a little more each month, became too tired to push the needle through the leather. The doctor ordered this and that. Selina sat up at night and often stayed away from the fields. Bill was sent here and there for medicines and delicacies. But none the less, when the hot weather came, Bobbie laid his weary head on the pillow, and smiled wistfully at Selina, and said, 'I'm tired, lass. I'll sleep a bit.'

And he slept on now under the ugly battened mound of brown earth. The pansies nodded golden heads as they did last year, the pig awaited the race with the same complacent ignorance as had the pig of last year.

Jakeways was rather shocked at this callousness of Selina's. 'I doubt it's no good to fly in the face of folk. It's the same in pleachin'—yo mun lay the bough the way it wants to go,' he said.

'Fine and pleased they be,' remarked Mrs. Marsh to the sexton's wife, 'and it wunna be above a month or so before there's a wedding in Cherrington.'

'She's a lucky woman, no danger!'

'Ah! A tidy chap. Keeps off the drink too. Never merry but of a Saturday night.'

II

Meanwhile the competitors were gathering for the most exciting race of the day. Even the Vicar and the Doctor drew towards the course to see the ladies distinguish themselves. The Vicar kept a deaf ear turned to the broad jokes and the betting among the young men, each of whom backed his own girl, speaking of her in racing terms.

The Doctor, knowing everybody's constitution to a nicety, was entrusted with the handicapping. He gave Mrs. Marsh a tremendous start, because he knew she had incipient dropsy. Nobody else knew it, however, so there was a general groan. Mrs. Marsh decided to glaze the Doctor's collars as no collars had ever been glazed. She stood far up the course, and the judge, at the winning-post, saw her round white face shining there like an argent shield. Jane, with her cheeks as suddenly red as those of a Dutch doll, and her neat black hair, also like a Dutch doll's, was heavily handicapped; and so were the half-dozen giggling village girls.

Behind all the rest stood Selina.

'You're not in the race, of course, Mrs. Stone,' said Dr. Pierce.

'Ah, sir, I be.'

He looked surprised. The Vicar was distressed.

'No, no, Selina! Think!'

'I be to run, sir.'

'It's not wise, Mrs. Stone,' murmured the Doctor.

'No, already there are strange rumours about,' said the Vicar. 'It would not take much to make them say you murdered poor Bob.'

Selina flung her head back with the air of a savage queen.

'What do I care if they do, saving your presence, sir! Let 'em talk till their tongues shrivel! I shanna hear 'em.'

'Ready!' shouted the starter.

The pig was placed in position by his owner's oddman, and firmly held in spite of expostulation. Mrs. Marsh took off her bonnet. So might Britannia, for some enormous conflict, temporarily doff her helmet. The girls flung their hats to their mothers or friends.

Selina turned to Jakeways with a smile of great sweetness and sadness. It came on her harsh face like dawn on a mountain side. It was clear from her smile that she loved him, but with an anguished love.

'I'm bound to run, lad,' she said.

There was in her voice the mournful note that the wind raises about the shell of ruined masonry, its lament around old dead cities, its cry in the cornices of abandoned homes.

'Ready—steady—go!'

The oddman let the pig go, and tumult broke over the course—yells from the various backers, squeals from the pig, hands held out to snatch, flying feet, laughter, fury.

'Selina runs as if life and all was on it.'

'I'll be bound she'll win.'

'Go it, Mrs. Marsh!' shouted the Doctor.

Like a nest of hungry birds, Jane's nephews and nieces lifted their voices—

'Keep at it, a'ntie!' Then, jubilantly, 'Mrs. Stone's fell down.'

'But she's got the pig,' wailed their mother.

Far up the course, with both arms round the pig, lay Selina. The roar of applause died away as she still lay there.

The crowd surged forward.

'It's a judgment.'

'Ah! She's strook.'

'Sarve un right.'

'Being so desper't set on a pig! And poor Stone not sodded!'

'Well, seems like she's done for herself now, no danger.'

'Struck down in 'er pride!'

'What is it?'

'What's took the woman?'

'Twas poor Bobbie Stone as come agen in the middle of the race and called 'er. They come agen very bad afore they're sodded, you mind.'

Meanwhile, by the silent Selina and the shrieking pig knelt the Doctor. She was coming round, but he knew the case was hopeless. It was heart–failure.

'You know what I told you after that influenza—about your heart, Mrs. Stone?'

'Yes.'

'You knew what would happen. Why take such a risk for a pig?'

'A pig? What pig?'

The Doctor was puzzled, but silent.

Jakeways elbowed through the crowd, and, seeing her deathly face, burst into tears. He knelt down and loosened her tense, unconscious fingers from the pig.

'There wunna no call for you to do it,' he said mournfully. 'I'd ha' seen as you'd enough o' meat, if you'd set up with me.'

'I know ye would.'

'I like ye right well, Selina.'

'And I like you. Only I was sore set on poor Bob. Baby an' all was Bob to me.'

Dr. Pierce returned with the Vicar. 'But if she didn't want the pig, what *did* she run for?' he was saying. 'Ask her, Vicar!'

The dreamy Vicar stooped and took her hand. Their eyes met, and understanding flashed from one to the other. Then Selina's heavy lids came down, and the only reply the Doctor ever had was her faint, enigmatic smile.

THE BREAD HOUSE

I

THE hut crouched upon the mountain flank, round and brown like a hedgehog. Above it, three miniature pine-trees, very old and heavy-topped, leaned to the east as the westerly gales dictated. In their dark masses all the winds, finding nothing else on the hill to resist them, thundered and lamented.

The hut, made of stakes and furze and thatched with bracken, became once every week a centre of life and gaiety. Here came Daniel Garner, commonly called Dan'l Breadman, riding his old white pony, the panniers on either side of the saddle stuffed with quartern loaves. And hither, by ones and twos, from hidden cottages in the hollows, came the hill folk to buy their weekly bread.

Daniel's silver hair was wild on the wind as the frosty hair of Time. He was an old man now, past seventy. But old as he was, he never missed his day, however savage the weather. Late sometimes, but always faithful, he was to be seen riding like an ancient Viking along the tops of the precipitous slopes. His voice, quavering but courageous, rose and fell amid the tumult like the voice of a storm-riding gnome, crying to his pony through the whistling of the bents:

'Now Jinny, my wench, tabor on a bit!'

When they came to a hillside like the slope of a roof, he would say briefly:

'Scrat up!'

On a day in February, when their shadows, of a faint bird's-egg blue on the cold snow, accompanied them with gentle obstinacy, Daniel broke open the frozen door, lit a fire of brushwood within, and set out his bread on a table made of fir logs. He made the bread himself, and he was proud of his handiwork, for it had the unvarying perfection of mastery. He could no more make a bad loaf than a stammering prayer.

Once a month he set aside business for an hour, spread a white cloth on the table, cut up one of his loaves, and administered the Sacrament to his customers. He was famed in the hills as the man who walked with God the day long.

The sign of his advent was the spire of blue smoke that went up from his old little chimney like a conjuror's plant, with a swift long stalk and a sudden flower.

'Breadman's come, mother!' would be the cry in the only cottage in sight, and a waved tablecloth, a small messenger or the tintinnabulation of a tray would convey the news to the next dwelling.

As Daniel stooped under the fir branches to pull out logs for the fire, the pine needles, each cased so thickly in ice that it was like a green streak in a prism, clashed faintly.

Frost had set in, hard and bitter, and seemed likely to endure for many weeks. But inside the fire blazed, the place was radiant with dancing daffodil light, and full of the splendid, clean smell of bread. The big cottage loaves stood shoulder to shoulder on the table, for to-day was not Sacrament day. Beside the loaves was Daniel's cash-box—a small red flower-pot.

Soon a customer arrived, and after a time about a dozen assembled. They were mostly old, bent men like Daniel, grave with the conscious upholding of the morals of the community—no light task in a community so primitive, where deeds flare up with the inconsequence of will-o'-the-wisps, and where passions, if momentary, are devastating.

'Come Friday, it'll be Sacrament agen, observed old Purkis of the moors. 'And the Lord grant a thaw by then, for my bones be weary of this bitter old frost.'

A thaw, to these benumbed children of the mountain, came near to symbolizing the very love of God.

The loaves gradually disappeared; the hobnail tracks that led up to the Bread House were matched by other tracks leading away from it. In the dark pine tree a thrush, that braved the winter there for the sake of Daniel's crumbs, settled itself fluffily for the night, and the frost strengthened its fortifications round the pine needles.

Daniel shook the pennies and sixpences and shillings out of his cash-box into his purse—an old sock tied with string. As he did so, he heard in the settled stillness of the outer cold the whirr of disturbed grouse, as though another customer was coming. As all his customers had been, Daniel was puzzled.

There was a crunching of footsteps on the hard snow, and a man entered.

'Dan'l Garner?' he asked in a velvet-soft sing-song, very different to the curt voices of the hill folk.

'Ah! Garner's the name I answer to, but most says Breadman.'

'Good names, good names! And him as wears 'em has a name also for chapel righteousness,' said the visitor caressingly.

'Well, well, neighbours will talk! But I didna think it had spread to strangers,' said Daniel, trying to keep the child-like pleasure out of his honest old face.

The visitor made no reply, but stooped and stirred the fire with a stick, so that the hut was all in a clear glow of saffron light.

Daniel was smiling, thinking—as when did he not?—of the treasure he was laying up in heaven, and of his savings, soon to be invested in a Paradisal security. For he was going to build, here where the Bread House stood, a chapel with a window of coloured glass, that would shine out on his arriving neighbours in wintry weather, and shine in on the earthen floor in summer. With the help of a carpenter who lived next door to him in the hamlet at the foot of the hill, where his bakery was, he could build a little one-roomed chapel very cheaply. The money was almost gathered together now. He had been saving for many years, and he was a bachelor and lived frugally. To his simple mind it seemed that by thus giving his all to God he would gain some sort of copyhold in those many mansions of which he loved to read—a tenement of everlastingness fronting the golden street, and inscribed in starry letters over the door with the name of Daniel Garner.

The visitor, smiling with a kind of elfin irony, drew from his pocket a small round mirror which he evidently used for vanity's sake, being a very handsome man, supple and well made. A bright handkerchief set off the sunburnt beauty of his face and throat. His small hands with their long fingers and black nails were brilliant with rings. His coat was fastened with two buttons of broken bone and three of solid gold. He seemed to keep within himself the vital, cynical brilliance of a diamond.

He crossed the room to Daniel with his easy, padding walk.

Daniel was thrown into an amazement by this strange creature.

'Look a' this'n!' said the young man, holding the glass before Daniel's own face.

He looked obediently but dreamily. For in the way of people who live much alone and nurse a single dream, he was apt to let outward things slip by him.

'Now,' ordered his guest imperiously, 'look a' *this'n!*'

Pointing to his own face with a splendid gesture, he struck an attitude.

Daniel looked, for the first time attentively, and his cry startled Jinny so that she plunged in the snow.

It was not on the rings and the gold buttons that Daniel's horrified eyes were fixed, but on the face, the beautiful face, before him—on the high brow, the speedwell-blue eyes, the large passionate mouth and long chin.

For the face of the young man was his own face, only different in expression. Daniel had the spiritual look that comes from long crushing of the flesh for the sake of an idea. The other was as soulless as a squirrel.

With a long, wild gaze the old eyes looked into the young ones across the declining firelight. The likeness to himself smote Daniel as the strong black arms of the pines smote the roof of the Bread House, violently, mercilessly.

'Can you mind,' said the suave voice, 'can you mind the Fair at Outspan six-and-thirty year ago come midsummer? Can you mind it, dear 'eart?'

He was as gentle as a cat with a mouse.

Daniel groaned.

'Eh, my soul, that night of nights the man as walks with God the day-long was as drunk as a Romany at a pony show.'

'Oh, the sin, the sin!' muttered Daniel. 'Forgive, Lord in Heaven! Ah, I was drunk that night. But never since—never since!'

'A righteous man was Daniel Garner that night, surely to goodness!'

'The past,' shouted Daniel, stung to wrath, 'is between my God and me!'

'And me, my dear,' purred the tormentor, disregarding the anger. 'Do you please to call to mind a well-favoured wench with yaller eyes that kept the cokernut shy?'

'Give over! Let be!'

'That was my mam … Dad!'

Daniel sprang up, goaded past endurance.

'The past be past. I've made confession to the Lord. It inna for you to give judgment.'

He looked with a kind of terror at the face he had brought into the world. His hands trembled and his face was ashen.

'I never thought—' he began.

'Never thought there was a chyild, a nice lickle chyild to comfort your old age,' suggested his son.

'The past is washed away.'

'I be the past!'

The stranger drew his body insolently to its commanding height, laughing with a flash of white teeth.

'And I be here.'

'What'n you want?'

'Now you talk straight talk. Now we understand each other, Dad.'

He spoke admiringly. The old man looked at him with an anxiety which pleased him.

'I heard talk, dear soul, of a lickle chapel, and a bag of money to build it with.'

There was a dreadful silence. Outside, Jinny fidgeted, for the cold strengthened, also she had eaten the only wimberry bush within reach, and there was a presage of snow, and she wanted to be home. She sighed.

'A tuthree pound for buttons,' went on the gentle ironical tones within, 'and a tuthree pound for rings, and the rest for a skewbald pony—a beautiful lickle pony!—and never a penny for the brick-and-mortar men.'

'No!' said the old man loudly. 'No!'

'If you dunna give it, Dad, I'll come whome along of you. I'll come with you when you bring the bread. I'll bide with you in lying down and in rising up. Folk only need to look at me to know, for I'm the very spit and image of my holy Dad. They wunna take the money. They wunna build the chapel. They'll turn you out for a sinner.'

Daniel knew it was true. If he did not manage to conceal this dreadful thing, his chapel would never be built. But neither could it be built if he gave up the money, for he was too old to save it over again.

'Well, Dad,' said the reasonable voice, 'I'll give you till next bread day to ponder it.'

'Sacrament Day!' muttered the old man.

'You can bring the bag of money then. Best come early, so nobody'll see me. When I've got it, I'll go.'

'Never will I bring it. Not till Doom breaks!'

They stared at one another hungrily, like two people who want the same loaf.

Then with a scintillating flash of eyes and rings and buttons the young man was gone.

When at last Daniel roused himself, locked the door, and untied Jinny, the snow was falling with a weighty softness, and night was upon them.

The old man swept a blue, tear-dimmed eye round the landscape. Grey freezing sky. Whining, clashing mountain trees.

'Bitter!' he murmured. 'A bitter old frost! Please God, send us a thaw!'

II

On Sacrament Day the door of the Bread House was open several hours earlier than usual, for Daniel wanted time to collect his thoughts, and to fortify himself for that which must happen.

He set out the white cloth and cut up the bread. His obstinate chin and long upper lip were fixed in changeless resolution. Come what might, his son should not have the money. He, Daniel, was going to lay it up before the Lord for ever, and the savour of it was to ascend to His nostrils like the good smell of new bread.

He had sent the money to his sister, a woman noted for piety, and the chapel was to be built in her name. He was quite determined that his son should not have a penny of it. He was going to tell him so, and let him do his worst. Then, disgraced but victorious, Dan'l Breadman would go forth into a wintry world.

Daniel had aged in these seven days. His hands shook like poplar leaves before rain. He felt the cold as he never had before, yet he forgot to light his fire.

The hurricane made a whirlpool of wind around the Bread House. In the wind, although the frost still held, was a presage of change.

Daniel crept about, making his preparations, with another roaring in his ears besides that of the wind in the pine trees. Sometimes this other roaring stilled and the wild beating in his left side, which seemed connected with it, sank to nothing, and he held to the table for fear of falling.

'I be mortal tired,' he said. He sat down by the table and rested his head on his arms. A great stillness fell upon the place.

Outside, the storm was less violent. The wind had crept round to the south. A faint thudding of water-drops began. The pine needles freed themselves from their icy cases. Snow slid from the Bread House roof. The sun came out, so that the rows of loaves shone ripely brown, and the flower-pot glowed like a bloodstone.

Silence met the young man's mocking voice. And when he tried to wake the sleeper, he could not. He saw upon his father's face a smile compounded of triumph, peace and mockery. Finding nothing to stay for, and being oppressed by the silence, he took the old man's watch and a few odd coppers, and went away.

Suddenly, from the topmost branch of the pine tree, the thrush that had wintered on Daniel's crumbs piped out to the limpid sky that the thaw had come.

THE NAME-TREE

CHERRY ORCHARD was for sale. The impossible thing, the thing that had yet threatened them always out of the misty future, had become fact. She could not believe it. She crouched under the lee of the sandstone wall of the garden, where the sun shone, for the spring wind was sharp and eager, and the slow, grinding poverty of years had worn all the wool out of her clothing. The beautiful old timbered house where she and her invalid father lived had consumed their small income as long as Laura could remember. She kept the place neat with her own hands, toiling in the vast, bare kitchen and in the wild, half-abandoned garden.

'I'd as lief,' she muttered, 'think of selling myself.'

The dark shadows under her eyes grew darker as a flush ran from chin to forehead, for she remembered—and would remember till the end of her life—the things Julius Winter had said to her yesterday.

Julius Winter was the new owner of Bitterne Hall. He had brought with him a wife almost as rich as himself, a Lady in her own right, and exactly like a pink sweet. Before Julius shone a vista of pleasant days with many smaller pink sweets about him.

Yesterday he had come with Lady Angela to return Laura's timid call—timid, because she never quite knew whether she was technically a 'lady' or not; whether she would be snubbed or not.

They had tea out of the depleted seaweed tea-set in the room that was so low and hollow-sounding, full of green light from the laurel outside the western window.

Lady Angela was tired.

'Laura, my dear,' said her father in his sad, disillusioned voice, which had faded since the advertisement of Cherry Orchard appeared, 'please show our guest the orchard.'

They went out through the French window, past the laurel that lifted its ancient, snakily twisted trunk almost to the casement window above, which was hers.

'This is my name-tree,' she said. 'Do you know the old belief about name-trees? If the tree dies, you die. If you sicken, the tree withers. If you desert it, a curse falls.'

'I can believe it, here.'

They came to the orchard. Roofed with pale ivory, heady with the thin, pure perfume of the cherry-blossom and of the cowslips in the dew-grey grass beneath, walled with apple-green to the east, where the tall hawthorn hedge had burst into leaf, and with black-green to the north, where a plantation of fir-trees held up white candles, the place lay wrapped in spells, dreaming its own dream.

It was the intolerable sweetness of it, of the sharp smell of crushed nettles, of the white cherry petals that wandered down the stirless air like tears, of the soft, pale cowslip calyxes, that shook her fortitude.

Beneath his questions, his instant perception, she sobbed helplessly, while his mocking, absorbed eyes dwelt upon her tear-blotted face.

'A cherry-flower in the rain,' he thought.

'Such passion for a place,' he said, 'is absurd.'

'Why?'

'Your love should be given to a man. Such passion as yours should bear fruit.'

She was silent.

'Is it race-memory? Because your ancestors loved it?'

'Maybe; but it goes further back than that.'

'Love of beauty?'

'No. I love the ugly things as much as the others. I'm as fond of the nettles as of the cowslips.'

'What is it, then?'

'It is that I've got roots here—the roots of my name-tree, and they go so deep. Did you hear this song, ever?

"She was born and bred with the birds.

Their words were her words.

For she was come out of the earth and water;

From lily leaf and ash bole.

She said, *I am the moaning forest's daughter,*

A tree hath my soul.

She slipped away between sunset and moonrise,

Between town hall and steeple,

Back to her own people.

Who knows where she wanders, where she lies?'"

She gleamed on him, and the light in her face astonished him. He had quite discarded the idea that she was posing. Lady Angela posed about the beauty of nature: but this woman was incapable of it. She had real, vital, savage passion in her fragile body. He had not thought passion of just that quality existed in the modern world. Certainly the women he had known had not possessed it. This woman had it, and she wasted it on a place. He watched her, standing slim and gauche, in her old brown dress, her soul tormented by love for something vague and mysterious, something he could not touch or name, that seemed to lie beneath the earthly beauty that she saw, like a dreaming god. Desire surged over him—the poignant longing that jonquils bring, the longing to touch the silken petals, to gather the brittle, faintly-scented stalks.

To possess this woman would be to ravish a forest.

Because he did not dare to touch her, he gathered a cowslip and ran his strong, dark fingers up and down its soft keys, bruising, breaking.

'Keys of Heaven,' she said. 'Every year I've watched them, from the first leaves, when the rooks were so loud in the March evenings, till the dry fruit.'

'Would you like to keep Cherry Orchard for ever?'

She looked at him, frowning.

'I will buy Cherry Orchard and give it you, if you will give me the keys of Heaven.'

'And Heaven is—?'

'Your love.'

The blossomy shadows lengthened. Somewhere in the elms beyond the orchard a pigeon moaned. Spiders went stealthily about their weaving, and the dew came with no sound upon leaf and flower. Still she was mute. It was as if the orchard expressed her mind. The dew fell. The dove mourned. The shadows lengthened.

'I have no love to give,' she said at last, 'to you or any man.'

'Before the fruit falls in your orchard,' he said, harsh and low, 'you shall give it to me.'

He cast one long look round the shadowy place. It was as if he gathered every tree into his arms.

She turned to the gate. This strange silence, full of the muttering of presage, terrified her.

They went back to the house, passing the old laurel.

'Your name-tree,' he said. He tore off a bunch of leaves in each hand, pressing them to his lips.

'Ah, you have hurt it! The curse will fall.'

He looked at her with the slow, ironical smile that Lady Angela dreaded. Then he held open the window for her to enter. And while his host made dignified protest against life and circumstance, the eyes of Julius brooded upon Laura, and saw in her lap the vision of a child—not a child like a sweet, but one compact of earth and dew, a child like a cherry flower. Before the fruit was set, Julius Winter began negotiations about the house. When the last faded cowslips were merged in the growing grass, he had bought it. Cherry Orchard, with its murmurs, its shadows, and its silences, was his.

Lady Angela, puzzled by this whim, said:

'It will do for Arthur.'

Arthur was their eldest.

Julius smiled. Then he laughed. There was something in his wife's remark that grew more amusing as he considered it. He could not imagine Arthur's small, round, complete entity presiding over that brooding place—that place where mists lingered and melodies sounded, and man wrestled with the spirit of earth.

'Arthur shall have it,' he said, 'if he can get it.'

'You mean, if you give it to him.'

'I can't give it to him.'

'Why?'

'I don't know why.'

'You are getting very strange in your manner, Julius. I believe it is that house. They tell me it is haunted.'

'Oh, it's haunted. I can vouch for that.'

At Cherry Orchard the old man said:

'It is the best that could have happened.'

'The best? Oh, you think it is the best?'

'The very best.'

She laughed; and her laughter, sad and wild as a frantic, imprisoned bird, beat on the rafters.

'You are very strange, my dear,' said her father.

When the rounded fruit softly acquiesced to ripeness, gathering gold and red in the midday sunshine; when the hay was cut and the long evenings thrilled with the singing of the swallows, Julius came every day, and the old man rejoiced to see his home being made so trim and weather-proof. Joy revived him, so that the illness which had held him loosened its grip. His voice lost its plaintive note.

'It is just as good as if it were my own again,' he said, 'with such a landlord.'

'With such a landlord!'

Her voice was full of little darts of fear and curiosity and scorn, that ran like lizards in and out of the words.

He came. As usual, they walked in the orchard after tea.

'The fruit is nearly ripe,' he said.

'Not yet.'

The trees brooded over them like jewelled birds in some ancient tapestry. They filled him with an ache of longing. He wanted to possess them, as a god might. He would possess them in her. His soul could only reach the outer fringes of hers; his voice strove to win her; his eyes burnt on hers, but she lowered her lashes and was mute. She remained aloof: but through the body he would reach her. She should have nothing of herself left, no corner of her spirit that was not his.

'I'll come for your answer this day next week, Laura. If it's no, you and your father will go at once.'

'And not see summer out?'

'And not see summer out.'

In one long, lingering look he took her face to himself, line by line, curve by curve.

'If it's yes—I know your window.'

So wild a gust of passion shook him that he left the place without another word, and came no more until the week was over.

'I'm glad you've finished at Cherry Orchard,' said Lady Angela. 'I'm sure the place is haunted. Still, perhaps it will do for Arthur.'

Moonlight was wan over Cherry Orchard, and the fruit shone, darkly polished, amid the soft, lulled leaves. The trees stood mute, quiescent in the pale light, and the laurel gave no faintest whisper as Julius and Laura passed it.

Once more they came to the orchard. Once more they stood beneath the great Morello tree.

'Ripe,' he said. 'Laura! Laura!'

She was silent. But a faint breeze, walking in the tree-tops, seemed to him to be her murmur of assent.

Only the sheer crudity of his desire for her, the strange universality of the mating he had willed, gave him courage to brave her white silence.

'To-night?' he said. 'Laura!'

Once again there fell from the tree-tops a vague, assenting murmur.

Laura wondered at her father, sitting in the western window, brisk and happy over his letters.

'I shall go to bed now, dear,' he said. 'But I had to write about the fruit. It is ripe.'

'Dead ripe,' said Laura.

She stood in the shadow of the laurel, and the large oval leaves seemed to be fingering her face.

She leaned from her window and saw the orchard huddled beyond its hedges like a flock at bay; saw the gables on the grass, and the ancient twisted trunk of the laurel climbing towards her window. In the faint airs the ivy breathed on the house like a living creature. In a meadow by the high road a corncrake, startled by some late traveller, set up its harsh crying.

Dawn, faintly reflected in the west, flowered in pale green and white, like an April orchard. Julius awoke. He wanted to shout in his ecstasy. He had imposed his being upon the white evanescence of a cherry flower. He had ravished the forest. Children minded like the forest should be his.

'Laura!' he whispered, 'I broke that old tree, I'm afraid; but Cherry Orchard is yours for ever.'

He stooped to kiss her, but she was dead.

MANY MANSIONS

HIS name—John Lloyd. His age—something verging on one hundred years. His home—a dusky cottage in an ancient borough. The cottage had one room below, very silent, full of shadows and soft lights from the low wood fire. An open staircase went up to the bedroom, so that when John Lloyd had supped, said his prayers and doused his fire, he could climb without much difficulty to his bed. In the corner by the fire stood his beadle's staff, painted in bands of black and yellow. For that ancient borough kept its old customs. It was a very Rip-van-Winkle of a borough. Somewhere in the Middle Ages it had fallen asleep, and if you should wonder at the fashion of its garments, you must remember that it had not, since the day it fell asleep, changed its coat, its hosen or its hat. So John Lloyd kept his staff, and in his hale years he would rap unruly lads on their round heads till you would think a woodpecker had come to church. Old folks, also, should they become too emotional in their prayers, did not escape his vigilant eye: but he would not touch them with his staff, only he would lay a reminding hand upon their shoulders. If the old lady whom he judged to have the right to communicate first was absorbed in prayer, he would gently insinuate his staff into her pew and give three little taps to her hassock. *Noblesse oblige.* She must not forfeit her prerogative, nor must she keep the congregation waiting.

But when I remember him, John was almost too feeble for his beadle's work. I was sent once a week as a small child to read the Bible to him. That was a great adventure! There was the walk of a mile down the country road, beside which ran a thread of a brook, except in the summer. In the hedgebanks grew a few sweet violets, and there you might find the largest, most brightly-coloured snail-shells I have ever seen. But one must not linger too long, for down there, in the pool of hyacinth made by the valley shadows and the gentle smoke of hearth fires, John Lloyd waited to hear about the Many Mansions.

On then, down the brown road between its sloping fields of miraculous green, past the roaring smithy, past—if possible—the small square window which had the splendid glass marbles. (But it could be passed if one remembered that the person who painted the marbles was really not half so good an artist as the person who painted the snail-shells.) Down the street of blue shadows, past the church with its needling spire, with just one glance through the wrought-iron gates beyond which lived a lady in a garden of lilies—the most beautiful of ladies she seemed to me, white and gold like her flowers, so that when I read to John Lloyd about Mary of Galilee pondering things in her heart, I always saw her beyond gates of wrought iron, walking in a garden of lilies. But this was seldom, because John liked what he called 'the Many Mansions piece,' and when it was his turn to choose, he chose that. And when it was my turn to choose, remembering that this was John's party, I was in honour bound to choose that also.

Up three hollow steps, into the dusky room, silent as one of the porches of eternity, and there was John in his Windsor chair, his black and yellow wand beside him, his great black Bible, so heavy that it made my arms ache, ready on the deal table.

'Come thy ways in, my dear,' he would say. 'And God be with ye. A grand morning, seemingly?'

'Grand, John. And here's a snail–shell in case you'd like a game of conker.'

'Nay, my dear, I be past conker. You keep it.'

'Then I'll put it in my faery house.'

'Ah. You do.'

'What shall I read, John?'

He made a great show of considering, saying, 'Well, there's a good few nice pieces. There's "The greatest of these." Then there's "The pitcher be broken at the fountain," and "I will give you rest." Then he would pause and in a moment say, as if it were a totally new idea:

'How about the Many Mansions piece, my dear?'

I had no need to look for it; the book always fell open just there.

'In my Father's house are many mansions.... If it were not so, I would have told you.'

John would strike his palm upon the table.

'Ah! Fair and square, He'd ha' told us,' he would say. 'If so be it was only a tuthree housen for the grand folk, and no room for us, He'd ha' said so, straight. But there's room for all, and He's gone to get it ready.'

'Shall you like going there, John?'

'Surely I shall, my dear.'

'Shall you go by train, or shall you get the cab from the *Arms*?'

He laughed at that, with a sound like the stirring of dry rushes.

'I doubt Tom Ostler would be put about to find that road.'

'Train, then?'

'No station!' said John tersely.

'Oh,' I said, 'I know! They're going to send for you!'

For I remembered how the lady of the garden once sent for me, and how I drove in unwonted glory past the violets and the snail-shells.

'Got it!' said John. 'Ah, they'll send.'

'A carriage?' I was glad for John.

'Horses of fire, and a chariot of fire!' said he, and the soft lights from the burning wood lit his old eyes to splendour.

'I'll come too!' I cried.

'You mun multiply by ten first.'

'How?'

'Ten tens a hunderd.'

'Wait for me, John!'

'Not to be done, my dear. They send when they've a mind.'

It is a long time now since they had a mind to send for John Lloyd, but I shall never forget the simple goodness of his seamy face, his inexpressive righteousness, his bantering affection.

PALM

SHE wandered through the square of tall, stern, dilapidated houses that might well be called Tower-of-Babel-Square. She cried out upon the silent, curtained windows of Bayswater. She reached forth a lean hand, gripping the arm of a woman passing by—

'Lady, O Lady! Buy a bunch of palm. I've walked so far, my dear, on these poor feet. See, lady! It is but March, and it's all budded beautiful. Buy a little bit, lady!'

Soon came the story. Ah, those old, woeful, laughter-bringing, everlastingly young stories of the London streets!

'It's my little girl, lady. O my dear, she's sixteen only, and don't be offended, lady, if I tell you. I'll whisper it. She courted a man.'

'Well, but so did Eve.'

'O my dear, but *she* didn't char. And he's gone away now. And she's a-lost her job owing to not being as she should. And if I don't stir about, she'll be brought to bed without so much as a shift. So I says, "I'll walk with palm. I'll walk till I drop, but she shan't be brought to bed without a shift." Spare me a shift, my dear, for the palm, and I'll take no money.'

With a bundle of linen for the little Madonna of the gutter she departed, leaving many blessings.

'She'll look right tidy in that, my dear. And a ribbon to tie up her hair as well. Gold hair she's got, and it was her ruin. When the One above gave women gold hair and little taking ways, He didn't mean well by 'em. Not if they chared where questions was asked. But thank you kindly, lady, and take a blessing from the child as is to come, and its mother and its grandmother. And may no child ever look darkly upon you!'

Her palm stands up against the pale wall, softly budded in pale silver. Spring is in it. Light lingers on it. Looking at the slender boughs, one sees again in Tower-of-Babel-Square, the weary woman lifting up her voice in the sweet twilight of early spring, to speak her daughter's confession and magnificat. And one is reminded of long, brown country roads, and of the voices, penetrating, obstinate and melodious, of the clover-breathing kine lowing after their young.

'IN AFFECTION AND ESTEEM'

MISS MYRTLE BROWN had never, since she unwillingly began her earthly course, received the gift of a box or a bouquet of flowers. She used to think, as she trudged away to the underground station every day, to go and stitch buttonholes in a big London shop, that it would have been nice if, on one of her late returns, she had found a bunch of roses—red, with thick, lustrous petals, deeply sweet, or white, with their rare fragrance—awaiting her on her table. It was, of course, an impossible dream. She ought to be glad enough to have a table at all, and a loaf to put on it. She ought to be grateful to those above for letting her have a roof over her head.

'You might,' she apostrophized herself, as she lit her gas-ring and put on the kettle, 'not *have* a penny for this slot. You might, Myrtle Brown, not *have* a spoonful of tea to put in this pot. Be thankful!'

And she was thankful to Providence, to her landlady, to her employer, who sweated his workers, to the baker for bringing her loaf, to the milkman for leaving her half a pint of milk on Sundays, to the landlady's cat for refraining from drinking it.

To all these, in her anxious and sincere heart, she gave thanks. She had enough to keep body and soul together. How dared she, then, desire anything so inordinate as a bouquet?

'You might,' she remarked, holding up the teapot to get the last drop, 'be sleeping on the Embankment. Others as good as you, as industrious as you, sleep there every night, poor souls.'

Yet she could not help thinking, when she put out her light and lay down, of the wonderful moment if she ever *did* receive a bouquet.

Think of unpacking the box! Think of seeing on the outside, 'Cut Flowers Immediate,' undoing the string, taking off the paper, lifting the lid!

What then? Ah, violets, perhaps, or roses; lilies of the valley, whiter than belief in their startling bright leaves; lilac or pale pink peonies or mimosa with its benignant warm sweetness.

The little room would be like a greenhouse—like one of the beautiful greenhouses at Kew—with the passionate purity of tall lilies; with pansies, softly creased; with cowslips in tight bunches, and primroses edged with dark leaves, and daffodils with immense frail cups. She would borrow jam-pots from the landlady, and it would take all evening to arrange them. And the room would be wonderful—like heaven. The flowers would pour out incense, defeating the mustiness of the house and the permanent faint scent of cabbage.

To wake, slowly and luxuriously, on a Sunday morning, into that company—what bliss!

Red roses at the bed's head, white roses at the foot. On the table, pinks. Not A *few* flowers; not just a small box. Many, many flowers—all the sweetness the world owed her.

She dimly felt that it owed her something. All those buttonholes! Yes. There was a debt of beauty. She was the world's creditor for so much of colour and perfume, golden petals, veined mauve chalices, velvet purples, passion flower, flower of the orange. She was its creditor for small daisies and immense sunflowers; for pink water-lilies acquainted with liquid deeps; for nameless blooms, rich, streaked with strange fantastic hues, plucked in Elfland; for starred branches dripping with the honeys of Paradise.

'Dr. to Myrtle Brown, the World. Item, love and beauty. Item, leisure. Item, sunlight, laughter and the heart's desire.'

She might, of course, out of her weekly wage, buy a bunch of flowers. She did occasionally. But that was not quite the perfect thing, not quite what she desired. The centre of all the wonder was to be the little bit of pasteboard with her name on it, and the sender's name, and perhaps a few words of greeting. She had heard that this was the custom in sending a bouquet to anyone—a great actress or prima donna. And on birthdays it was customary, and at funerals.

Birthdays! Suppose, now, she received such a parcel on her birthday. She had had so many birthdays, and they had all been so very much alike. A tomato with her tea, perhaps, and a cinema afterwards. Once it had been a pantomime, the landlady having been given a ticket, and having passed it on in consideration of some help with needlework.

Miss Brown liked the Transformation Scene. She liked the easy way in which the ladies who had been reclining on sharp, green peaks of ice in a snowbound country were suddenly, at the ringing of a bell, changed into languid, rosy summer nymphs with as many blossoms about them as even she could desire. She supposed they were only paper flowers and trees of cardboard, but still it would be pleasant to recline in a warm rosy light and see rows and rows of pleased faces. Yes. If she had been younger, she might have become a transformation fairy. She mentioned this when thanking the landlady for a pleasant evening.

'What? Go as one of those brazen girls? Dear me, Miss Brown, what next?'

'They only just lie there in a nice dress to be looked at,' said Miss Brown, with spirit.

'There's some,' replied the landlady darkly, 'as do more harm, just lying still to be looked at, than respectable people would do in a thousand miles.'

'I'm not young enough, anyway.'

'No. You don't get any younger. Time soon passes.'

She minced the meat for the first-floor dinners as if Time and Death were on the chopping-board.

Myrtle Brown was depressed at the idea of Time and Death marching upon her. She realized that there would come a time when she could not make any more buttonholes. She knew she ought to be saving every penny against the rainy day which, once it came, would go on. Even a bunch of snowdrops would not do.

'There'll come a day,' she said, as she washed her cup and saucer after a frugal tea, 'when you'll *want* a penny, when a penny may be life or death. Save, and be thankful!'

Yet always in her heart was the longing for some great pageant, some splendid gift of radiance. How she could enjoy it! With what zest she would tell over every smallest bit of it! Nothing that they could give her would go unnoticed. Every petal, every leaf would be told over like a rosary.

But nobody seemed anxious to inaugurate any pageant. Nobody wanted to light a candle at Miss Brown's shrine. And at last, on a bleak winter day when everything had gone wrong and she had been quite unable to be grateful to anybody, she made a reckless decision. She would provide a pageant for herself. Before she began to save up for the rainy day, she would save up for the pageant.

'After that,' she remarked, carefully putting crumbs on the window-sill for the birds, 'you'll be quiet. You'll be truly thankful, Myrtle Brown.'

She began to scrimp and save. Week by week the little hoard increased. A halfpenny here and a penny there—it was wonderful how soon she amassed a shilling. So great was her determination that, before her next birthday, she had got together two pounds.

'It's a wild and wicked thing to spend two pounds on what neither feeds nor clothes,' she said. She knew it would be impossible to tell the landlady. She would never hear the last of it. No! It must be a dead secret. Nobody must know where those flowers came from. What was the word people used when you were not to know the name?

'Anon'—something. Yes. The flowers must be 'anon.' There was a little shop at Covent Garden where they would sell retail. Tuberoses, they sometimes had. Wonderful things were heaped in hampers. She would go there on the day before her birthday.

'You ought,' she said, as she drank her cup of cocoa at five o'clock on a winter morning, 'to be downright ashamed of what you're going to do this morning. Spending forty shillings on the lust of the eye!'

But this rather enhanced the enjoyment, and she was radiant as she surveyed early London from the bus.

To-morrow morning, not much later than this, it would arrive—the alabaster box of precious nard.

She descended at Covent Garden, walking through the piled crates of greenstuff, the casks of fruit, the bursting sacks of potatoes, the large flat frails of early narcissi, exhaling fragrance. She came to her Mecca.

The shopkeeper was busy. He saw a shabby little woman with an expression of mingled rapture and anxiety.

'Well, ma'am, what is it?' he asked. 'Cabbage?'

Cabbage! And she had come for the stored wealth of a hundred flower-gardens!

'No, sir!' she replied with some asperity. 'I want some flowers. Good flowers. They are to be packed and sent to a lady I know, to-night.'

'Vi'lets?'

'Yes. Vi'lets and tuberoses and lilies and pheasant-eye, and maidenhair and mimosa and a few dozen roses, and some of those early polyanthus and gilly-flowers.'

'Wait a minute! Wait a minute! I suppose you know they'll cost a pretty penny?'

'I can pay for what I order,' said Miss Brown with hauteur. 'Write down what I say, add it up as you go on, put down box and postage, and I'll pay.'

The shopkeeper did as he was told.

Miss Brown went from flower to flower, like a sad-coloured butterfly, softly touching a petal, softly sniffing a rose. She was bliss incarnate. The shopkeeper, realizing that something unusual was afoot, gave generous measure. At last the order was complete, the address given, the money—all the two pounds—paid.

'Any card enclosed?' queried the shopman.

Triumphantly Miss Brown produced one.

'In affection and esteem.'

'A good friend, likely?' queried the shopman.

'Almost my only friend,' replied Miss Brown.

Through Covent Garden's peculiarly glutinous mud she went in a beatitude, worked in a beatitude, went home in a dream.

She slept brokenly, as children do on Christmas Eve, and woke early, listening for the postman's ring.

Hark! Yes! A ring.

But the landlady did not come up. It must have been only the milkman. Another wait. Another ring. No footsteps. The baker, she surmised.

Where was the postman? He was very late. If he only knew, how quick he would have been!

Another pause. An hour. Nothing. It was long past his time. She went down.

'Postman?' said the landlady, 'why, the postman's been gone above an hour! Parcel? No, nothing for you. There did a parcel come for Miss Brown, but it was a great expensive box with 'Cut Flowers' on it, so I knew it wasn't for you and I sent it on straight to Miss Elvira Brown the actress, who was used to lodge here. *She* was always getting stacks of flowers, so I knew it was for her.'

Owd Blossom

NOBODY knew his real name. Nobody wanted to know it. He had always been just 'Owd Blossom'; always been considered simple. At the farms where he worked, his ungainly movements, his clumsy, unhandy ways could always be relied on to raise a laugh. He was very long and thin and knobby; his face went in where it should have gone out, and he wore a perpetual and rather fatuous smile. Beneath the smile, into the grave, wistful soul of the man, nobody ever thought of looking. Even the Vicar had never suspected Owd Blossom of complete sanity. People said he had an unket look, with his wispy hair and rheumy eyes. Then there were the flowers he always wore, from which he was named. Winter and summer, he had a posy, sometimes a flower-show of posies. His decorations varied from a single snowdrop in his buttonhole to a wreath of red roses in his hat, from an ear of wheat arranged as a tiepin to a shoulder-knot of mistletoe. He picked them mostly in the hedges, for he did not possess a garden, and the only time he could pluck red roses was when he gathered for market at the farms. He was happy on those days, and he would murmur, without any envy or malice, 'It's very pleasant for folks as owns a gyarden.'

Ridicule he met by the simple statement of his creed: 'I like a flower.'

He lived in a disused barn in the middle of the foldyard at Wainham's. On Sunday afternoon, before he went to litter-down the stock for the night, he would lean over a gate, or lie on the hillside, and brood upon the plain. Nothing ever came of his broodings; at least, there was never anything for anyone to see. He would shake back his flaxen hair, chew a stalk of bracken and murmur, 'I like a sunset.' That was all.

The farmers' wives were kind to him, for farmers' wives, perhaps from their continual care of small creatures, have motherly souls. They did not stint him in food or flowers, and when he gazed dumbly into the sunset or the flowering trees, they only said tolerantly, 'It's sad for the poor gwerian to have neither house nor child, nor flocks nor folk. It inna his fau't as the Almighty made him simple.'

Year after year, as the seasons shed their gold and purple, their rose and scarlet, on the pale shores of time, Owd Blossom absorbed them. He was like some pilgrim strayed into the great hospitable hall of a castle, who, finding the feast outspread with wine and fragrant bread, and minstrels singing in the glow of the faggots, forgot his pilgrimage and shared in the feast with silent gratitude.

Sometimes he would gently stroke the deep-coloured petals of a rose or a violet, or the round red cheek of little Daisy, the youngest of the Wainhams, and his caress was received confidingly, by flower and child.

Daisy loved him, and his dog idolized him. His dog was just the kind of animal you would expect him to possess. Everything about it was unexpected, queer. Its ears were wrong. Its colour was wrong. It lolloped. It was irretrievably ugly and utterly mongrel. They lived together in the whispering barn, keeping the feast of Christmas in great state by the glowing forge in the lower story, and making merry with such food as had been given to them. And if the kind Madonna of the old pictures, whose face is so motherly and sad and sweet, could have looked in on their revelry, she would certainly have stepped through the dark, starry window of the loft above and spread her rich blue robes on the straw, and given them her blessing between a smile and a tear.

Once Owd Blossom won a dubious celebrity by breaking his leg in saving this same mongrel—Tinker by name.

'Ah, well,' was the verdict of the farmhouse supper-table, 'if we 'adna known you was a poor simpleton, we'd know it now. Break your leg for a dawg!'

He simply smiled his old smile and said, 'I like a dawg.'

Tinker loved him better than ever, if that were possible. The seasons washed on over the sounding shores of time. Owd Blossom's hair paled from flaxen to white, like a hank of dyed wool left out in all weathers. He continued to gather for market, to feed the engine at threshing time, to litter-down the stock, to brood upon beauty, and to possess nothing but a dog that nobody else wanted.

Little Daisy grew taller and sweeter, till she stood in the vast, hushed, echoing porch of womanhood. She was so sweet that in a little while—in no time at all, as it seemed to Owd Blossom—she was spoken for, promised, and shouted in church. When she had been shouted three times, so Owd Blossom understood, she would be married.

Tinker and his master sat up late in the evenings, creating a wedding present. It was a box to keep salt in, and it was covered with pine-cones, varnished very splendidly. Tinker rolled the pine-cones towards his master, looked for rats in the box, and gave to the undertaking his whole-hearted sympathy. They saw, every green and golden summer evening, Daisy going to meet her lover across the wave-like undulations and dimples and shadows of the fifty-acre field, which was commanded by the window of their loft. Sometimes Daisy started too early, and then she would sit on the grass and pull the petals from her name-flower and say:

'He loves me; he loves me not.'

Or she would gather wild roses and bedeck herself, singing. Her lover always came at the same time, for haying had not begun, and he came straight from his work at six. Owd Blossom and Tinker liked to watch her, so the salt-box progressed slowly. It was through this long, loving vigil of his that Owd Blossom saw, on a clear-coloured evening between Daisy's first and second shouting, something that made him start from his seat and stare away to the farthest corner of the big field down where the stream made a pool. The stream ran from top to bottom of the field, and half-way up, where the path cut across it at right angles, was a spring. At the spring was Daisy. What was that by the pool down yonder?

Owd Blossom sprang for the ladder with a curse; through the foldyard he went, and out into the fifty-acre meadow with Tinker, gay and eager, at his heels.

What had his master seen to make him run so, to make him sweat so, and grunt in his running? Anyway, it was the best gallop they had ever shared.

'Oh, Lord!' muttered his master, and then he beckoned to Daisy and called:

'Come back, little Daisy! Go whome! There's the black bull from Bitterley down meadow!'

Daisy, with panic in her feet, fled past them, pale and gasping. For the black bull from Bitterley had 'savaged' two men with pikels last time he broke pasture. He had killed several dogs and nearly killed a cowman. As she passed them, she cried out in a sob: 'Johnnie!'

Owd Blossom had turned to follow her. He was exceedingly glad the gate and the farm were so near. He would fetch the Wainhams' men and Daisy's father with his gun. He had seen the bull lift his head from the pool and turn slowly to take his proud course up the field to the spring where the water was fresher. Soon he would stand beside the path—right in the way of Daisy's lover.

At that agonized cry of 'Johnnie!' Owd Blossom stopped. Intense concentration made him look more stupid than ever.

There was no way round. The field stretched its folded and dimpled acres, yellow with buttercups, on either hand. Daisy's lover would be in it now, striding across a little valley that lay beside the far fence. He would not see the bull until long after it had winded him, for its course lay in the valley where the stream was, and the wind was blowing straight for the stream, from the south, behind Johnnie.

If Owd Blossom followed Daisy, she would have no lover to meet across the meadows to-morrow. Even now he might be too late. He could see nothing of the bull nor of Johnnie, because of the undulations in the land.

To turn back in cold blood. To die. Not to finish the salt-box. Not to gather for market any more, nor brood on any more sunsets. The thoughts went round in his head like tadpoles in a pond. His hat-wreath of wild roses hung crookedly.

'Tinker!' he said.

Tinker made himself into half the letters of the alphabet.

'Whome, Tinker!'

His beloved friend should not be torn to ribands on those cruel horns.

Tinker was mutinous. His eyes said: '*You* are home.'

Why should he go away out of the sound of this voice, out of this comfortable presence?

'Whome, curse yer!' shouted his master, and turned from the fleeing figure and the painted west against which were set the farm chimney-stacks, dark and solid and pleasant, with pale smoke from the supper fire trailing from one of them.

'Daisy! Little Flower!' muttered Owd Blossom, as he lolloped on with his falling wreath of roses, running as fast as he could to meet the black bull from Bitterley.

The story should end here, but it cannot. If it did, Love would be left for ever facing Death, and nobody would know whether the salt-box was finished, or whether Daisy met her lover in the fifty-acre meadow again.

She did. For she ran so fast for help that when Johnnie found the bull standing over Owd Blossom and tore a great branch of the oak tree by the spring to keep him at bay, the Wainhams' men were already in the field. Tinker behaved with gallantry, and they carried Owd Blossom home with a kind of reverence. And because he was very tough and very case-hardened he managed not to die. So the salt-box was finished. And Daisy's lover took two small cottages instead of one big cottage. In the second lives Owd Blossom, with a garden of his own, meeting all questions about his bravery as he met those about his foolishness.

'I like a flower,' he says.

CAER CARIAD

A Story of the Marches

I

IN the Red Valley were only two houses—that of Zedekiah Tudor, ferociously scarlet, and that of his God, coldly grey. The valley, bird-scorned since Zedekiah had lopped the trees and pleached the hedges, would have been mute but for the dark music of the weir, lamenting.

It was a bitter night when Zedekiah stood with Dinah, his wife, in the graveyard. They were hidden, except for occasional greenish moonlight, in inky gloom. When the moon tore suddenly through the driving wrack, the shadows of the graves seemed to Dinah to spring at her like creatures out of ambush. The wind drove down the valley, howling, and Zedekiah spoke even more loudly than usual.

'Woman, confess yer sin, by the chyild's grave!'

Dinah's face, floating up momentarily out of the darkness, quivered, looking in the moonlight like a green-tinted white flower on black water. She was afraid of Zedekiah and of his God, and of the ghostly child that had scarcely breathed and had attained for her superstitious mind in the last six months a kind of ghoulish entity. She dreaded hearing Zedekiah mention David, her lover, and tarnish with his thoughts her new, mysterious joy. Her look of anguish revealed, as such looks do, the depths of expression underlying her usual one, and Zedekiah might have seen that her love story was not on the plane he imagined. But, as the local pig-sticker, he could hardly be expected to indulge in the finer emotions; and being, as he said, outside prop and inside pillar of religion in the Red Valley, he knew that all men are vile, altogether born in sin.

'There wanna no sin, Zedekiah.'

'Dunna lie. You were along of the man, yea, many a time, in the spinney.'

'There wanna no fau't.'

'If there'd a' bin no fau't, what for did you go with un?'

Dinah was silent. How could she explain what was mysterious even to herself—mysterious and wildly sweet? How could she show Zedekiah that David was her spirit's young companion, lover of that remote self in her which dwelt, silent and hitherto alone, far beyond the little noise of daily life? Even if she could have expressed these things, how could Zedekiah understand David? For David was one of those changelings sometimes found in hard, respectable, prosperous communities. He had an eager brain, emotions, a love of beauty, belief in impulse. He had shaken himself free of views such as Zedekiah held on religion, sex, and money. In the new, thrilling intimacy of the last two months there had simply been no time for the things that Zedekiah suspected. She realized wearily that it was no use trying to explain.

'In times gone by you'd a' stood in a sheet for it, a woman as was a sinner.'

'We on'y wanted to be together, Zedekiah; we'm clemmed each for other. And it inna our fau't as David come too late; if he'd a' come when you did, I'd a' chose him.'

This quiet putting of him in a lower scale than David enraged Zedekiah. It was a blow to his vanity that he never forgave.

'You'd follow the wastrel like a bitch,' he snarled.

She crouched on the grave, cowed, as are all sensitive temperaments, by the unbelievable coarseness and crassness of the world. She knew suddenly that her one desire was to follow David to the world's end, that so she would attain holiness. Yet how could that be, since she would be breaking the laws of God and man?

Instinct told her that David was beautiful and good, Zedekiah ugly and evil. Impulse cried, 'David!' across the waste places of her life. But tradition, herd-morality, were too strong for the new impulse. The night was dark, David absent, Zedekiah and his God imminent; and from the graves, threatening and grisly, she heard the dead preaching their dead creed. Superstition held its victim. She was bound to Zedekiah. She had married him because it was expected of her, and because the institution of marriage was the only respectable vocation open to her. On her wedding night she had feared him. When, at daybreak, satisfied and bland, he had recited the Magnificat, she had hated him. When her child was born she had cried out that it was a text and not a child that she was bringing into the world. When it died after three weeks she was not very sorry.

Zedekiah's voice rose harshly above the grievous water and the gentle sea-murmur of the larches in the spinney beyond the valley.

'Swear! Swear you'll ne'er see un agen in the face o' flesh!'

The water cried out like a soul in prison. It had come from afar; it journeyed into mystery; it chafed at the forbidding banks of Zedekiah's valley.

'Oh, I canna! I canna!'

'Swear or burn.'

'But there's nought wicked in giving David good-day.'

'It wouldna be only good-day as you'd give un.'

Dinah knew, with feminine shrewdness, that Zedekiah's words had a germ of truth, that some day the fire of physical love must leap up between her and David. This put her in the wrong. She had been brought up in the demonology that Zedekiah professed. She believed in his terrible devil, his yet more terrible God.

'Where their worm dieth not,' shouted Zedekiah. 'Swear!'

She moaned. To her an oath was unbreakable, and her love for David was a fierce, primitive thing, as are all spiritual needs.

'It's not as I want you,' said Zedekiah; 'it's what the neighbours 'ud say; and the saving of your soul.' He added this as an afterthought. 'Here I am, ready to forgive the sin and take yer back.'

'But I dunna want to come back! It's David I'm fond on.'

The darkness hid the rage in Zedekiah's close-set black eyes.

'If you swear to-night,' he said persuasively, 'you'll maybe save him as well.'

Dinah thought of the town of Heaven, full of people singing part-songs without wrong notes or practice; she and David would be able, in the general stir, to slip away somewhere and be at peace. She joined the multitudes that sacrifice life to eternity.

'I swear!' she said, and slipped down in a heap on the cold, unfriendly little grave.

II

Dinah stood at the door of the Red House and looked down the valley. Nothing had changed, although forty-five years had passed over it since the wild night of her vow. Four more cold little graves had been added to the first, for Dinah's children had been stillborn.

Zedekiah had let it be tacitly understood that they died because the Lord was angry with Dinah, and as Zedekiah was a religious man everyone believed him. So an impregnable wall of prejudice rose around Dinah, imprisoning her, shutting her away from sympathy. Every Sunday, in the house of their God, the small congregation eyed her stonily. Coming out on dark winter nights, it seemed to Dinah that the eyes of her unbreathing children followed her with the same sneering coldness as did the eyes of Zedekiah's grandmother, whose portrait (done in plentiful oils, and unforgivably like Zedekiah) hung in the parlour. Dinah watched this portrait every evening, when, with his small eyes shut and his long, inquisitive nose pointing toward the hearth-rug, Zedekiah prayed aloud that she might be forgiven, while the tree-tops in the spinney kept up their inward, promising music, all unheeded.

Zedekiah felt that he had been very forbearing with Dinah; he had never forgiven the wound to his vanity, and whenever she shrank from him he was silently furious. He expressed his anger in a scheme of daily petty tyrannies, under which Dinah grew yearly more feckless and spiritless, coming at last to believe that only by lifelong penitence could she save her soul. The house pressed upon her with its hideous comfort, and the water, clamant in the night, had a summoning tone. Ten years ago, she had been called simple; now she was openly spoken of as a *gwerian*. Zedekiah ceased to regard her as worthy of his supervision. Free for the first time, she began to wander. She was so mentally inert that she had a kind of kinship with inanimate things, and they began to murmur and mutter in her ears. She had lost the sanity of others, which had been her madness, and now that men called her mad she drew near to the patient reason of nature.

As she stood—a small, bent figure—in the pretentious doorway with its surrounding brickwork of yellow and red, she felt a stirring in her mind of something almost approaching to impulse. The April day was like the underside of a waterfall. Green rain was blown in glassy gusts along the blue lower slopes of the hills and through their far-flung shadows. Another green rain of soft needles hung in the larches, whose tops just showed above the high ground that closed the valley. It was as if they grew in a submerged country, an enchanted country lying deep in mist and magic. Dinah had not been to the spinney since her last meeting with David.

'I've a mind to go,' she said to herself. She fetched her shawl and set off. The spinney, when she pushed the white wicket open and entered, dripped and burned with light.

She wandered, mazed, into its heart, and saw how the soft golden chalices of the Lent lilies dipped and rose among their green spears—how they shone down the long slopes under the larches—how they caressed each other, flower on soft flower, sleek leaf on leaf. She gathered a handful and buried her lined face in them, breathing their vast, vague freshness—healing and tear-compelling—while all about her, with a hushed fairy clamour, the finches sang. It was then, brought by some green charm, that the full flood of madness—as the neighbours would have called it—came upon Dinah. Intuition was awake. She had unconsciously, by virtue of complete passivity, reached the state which the mystic attains consciously. And from the secret centre of the radiant day her message came. She, who had cowered so long, stood up straight in the ardent warmth; she gazed up into the pure, pale sky, and her grey eyes shone suddenly with love and joy. Then she spoke, and her voice, quavering but confident, dominated by its undernote of ecstasy the mysterious, lifting murmur of the tree-tops and the delicious hilarity of the finches.

'I be clemmed for David. I be going whome to David, and You can send me to the Bad Place if You've a mind!'

There did not seem to be any criticism in the bright world—all made of amber and green and pale blue glass—as she left the spinney and set forth with a brave heart on her twenty-mile walk. She would find her way, she was sure, to the tiny cottage that was David's own, where he dwelt under the southern slopes of Caer Cariad. She knew exactly, for David had told her, how it looked and where it stood—long dreamed of, long desired.

By mossy tracks where primroses bloomed in bridal bouquets; through grave beech-woods transparently roofed with young leaves; over the quick, pointed grass that pricked up, thick and wet, through a powder of daisies with delicate elation; across the brown, rounded hills she passed, grotesque and sombre. When horses galloped or bullocks bellowed in roadside fields, her timid heart leaped fearfully, but she kept on.

What would David be doing when she got there? 'Setting taters, likely,' she thought. She wondered what he would say. It did not occur to her to wonder how he would look. In the late afternoon shadows she came, faint and stiff, to the brow of a hill overlooking a great stretch of country. Wind-tormented may-trees embowered her. They were breaking into blossom, and their fresh green was jewelled with curd-white buds. She did not know that she herself, gnarled and stricken as their ancient trunks, outshone their budding promise by the sudden white flowering of her spirit. She was absorbed in contemplation; for there, across the Paradisal land that ran thick with evening's honey, standing in sweet and homely majesty on a crest of rose and pearl, was Caer Cariad. As she shaded her eyes she could see, nestling in its lower woods, a cottage, small and creamy as a hawthorn flower. It was far away indeed, but it was there, and it was David's. It beckoned her. Mile after mile the willing old feet trudged on. But now came the fear that always dogs fulfilled desire. Maybe David would not want her; he might be married; she had not thought of that. He might be gone away. To keep down the darkest thought of all she began to sing, and her cracked, plaintive voice sounded strangely in the gathering dusk.

It was dark when she climbed, sick with exhaustion, up the steep garden to the cottage door. The neglected borders, the windows, uncurtained and unlit, almost stopped her low pulses. Was there to be any welcome for her in the dark house? Was not the fire dead on the hearth, the singing–bird dead in the window?

She knocked and waited, while from the last purple summit of Caer Cariad the light lapsed.

Then, low and rich with promise of love past the bargaining loves of the world, there came on the quiet scented air the voice of David, the voice of the beloved—

'Come thy ways in!'

But when Dinah stood in the doorway she saw, not the David of her dreams, but an old man—white-haired and feeble—crouching over a low wood fire in a neglected and disordered room. And suddenly all the triumph of attainment, the joy of the imagined meeting, died within her.

'Life gone by!' she said, 'and I met a' been along of you. Life gone by!'

'Why, Dinah, my dear!'

David spoke soothingly. He asked no questions, showed no surprise. A sense of peace began to steal over Dinah. She surveyed the table, stacked with unwashed china; the grey ashes in the grate; the tiled floor—of a uniform mud-colour; the grease-covered candlestick in which David had just lit the candle.

'You didna get married, then?'

'It dunna look much like it.' David smiled humorously at his own expense. 'I got on pretty tidy till I took ill,' he explained.

'And never-a-one to do for you?' she asked, torn between the wish that he should have been comfortable and a fierce jealousy of any other woman who should have dared to look after him.

'I couldna take up with any but you, Dinah.'

'An' now I've come and I'm only an ugly old woman!' cried Dinah in misery.

'Dunna you dar' say it! And you wi' such pretty eyes! Didna I allus say you'd got pretty eyes?'

'Ah!'

The syllable expressed a whole world of content. There was no one else, and she was not ugly to him. All was well. Her eyes began to rove round the room possessively.

There crept into them the joy of battle, of creative art. Her fecklessness was gone, and excitement had overcome weariness.

'Afore I sleep,' she announced, 'I be going to clean the place, grate and quarries an' all. And I be going to wash up!'

She fell upon the disorder, and David, moving his chair from point to point, followed by the silently protestant cat, watched her with awed amusement. Never had an old woman worked with such fury, with such joy. She was labouring with her own hands for her beloved; she wanted no other Paradise. When at last, hours later, she brought the supper-table to the hearth in the clean, firelit, toast-scented room, and they sat hand in hand contemplating the Lent lilies in a jam-pot, he said—

'The place be all a-blossom, my dear, now as you've come.'

'I've broke the vow to come, lad, and I'll go to the Bad Place, but I dunna care.'

'I'm thinking the only Bad Place is minding what we met a' done each for other when it be too late,' said David. 'And I'm thinking Caer Cariad's a long way on to Paradise—a long way on it is.'

BLESSED ARE THE MEEK

THE workhouse dozed in the Sunday afternoon hush. In the old women's room all was very quiet; only a single bee groped clumsily up and down the shut windows, seeking the free air, flowers, the sounding hives.

The gloomy July afternoon laid an atmosphere of disillusionment over everything. The sky was of the same sad grey as the workhouse stockings. Ninety-eight feet, clad in these stockings, were posed in various attitudes down the long room, swinging, tapping, crossed, or set out stilly side by side like those on tombs.

Forty-nine women, dressed in decent Sunday garments with white aprons, sat in rows on benches facing one another. Forty-nine souls, varied and strange and wistful, clamant for delight as the bee, were shut in here. All these life-stories, full of sad and joyous and wild happenings, had stopped here, and were only waiting for Death to break the final thread. Life was over. They were conscious of it, dumbly, uncomplainingly. They could not have been more completely sundered from their past lives if they had died and gone to Purgatory. But every heart, in this house that was not home, kept, clear and changeless, the picture of the home it had lost; garden, shippen and fold; all the small, precious, sacramental things surrounding their busy lives— things they had hardly known to be precious until they were lost. For in those homes they had been individuals, centres of warmth and love. Here they were herded in a cold, almost derisive comfort; and through the long grey corridors the feet of the flame-clad, the laughter-bringer, the tear-giver—Love, were seldom heard.

They were knitting more grey stockings to wear when the others should be worn out. Their balls of wool, all exactly the same, lay beside them, and a blue-eyed kitten, passionately in love with itself, raced up and down the lines of passive feet and bullied the stout, unresisting balls.

'I'd lief be you!' said Fidelia Thatcher, who sat—tall, emaciated, white-capped—at the window end of a bench.

'That's a wicked imagination, Fidelia!'

This came from a neighbour, a stout, rosy old woman.

'Cats 'anna got souls,' she added.

Fidelia raised mild eyes, and her sweet, obstinate mouth took a firmer line as she said:

'Soul or no, I'd lief be that kit-cat.'

Her face, tanned golden by decades of suns and snows, had the dignity of an ancient Egyptian bas-relief. And though her long upper lip, high forehead, and arched nose were intimidating, her eyes—dark and dovelike, brooding upon the furiously energetic kitten and the anxious bee—were beautiful as the eyes of a heifer. Her large hands, twisted and swollen at the knuckles from years of work, lay quietly in the white union apron. She dreamed herself into the past. She was desperately afraid that in this place she might some day cease to believe in that past—in all the blossomy days that stretched away backwards from the day of her entrance here to her clover-scented childhood. To forget them would be like breaking faith with a lover.

One casement below and one above. What could a lone woman have wanted more? A pink rose-tree, a white rose-tree, and a lilac. These had presided over her garden. The white lupins had grown as tall as herself, and stood beside the wicket in pale dignity, like swordless angels. Her pigeons sunned themselves on the roof and paraded the tiles with soft pink feet. And, hearing the pattering enthusiasm of those pink feet above her attic morning by morning, and seeing the round cheeks of the roses pressed so confidingly against her window, she had almost forgotten that none would ever call her mother. Ah! Where was it now, that warm, scented peace? Where were those glad, laborious days when she scrubbed and rinsed the buttermits at the farm, returning in the evening with her perquisites of milk or pork or butter, with her small wage and her large content, and having her simple supper while dusk fell and the owls began to stir?

No conqueror of the world ever fought a harder, a grimmer battle, than Fidelia's battle against Fate—against hunger and the grey defeat that was its alternative. She had 'clemmed' and she had sweated. It was over now. She sat, a shade among shades, neither in Hell nor Heaven.

She rose and let out the bee. At the sudden cessation of its note the atmosphere grew more tense and heavy.

'Theer!' she said. 'Out o' prison.'

'Prison? What for, "prison"?' asked a flat-faced, meek woman. 'We gets our bellyful and a bed.'

'What's meat?' cried Fidelia suddenly, out of her bitterness. 'What's meat, with no heart to eat it? What's sleep with naught to wake for in the morning light?'

Down the benches ran a rustle and a sigh, like the wind in old, dry-leaved trees. There were murmurs.

'That's Gospel!'

'That's the righteous truth!'

'Delia's i' the right, no danger!'

With faces turned towards her as to a prophetess, they took courage to remember the days gone by. Those days, those homes, those fields, those dear lost faces shone in their souls with the peculiar lustre that mingled love and tears give to the human memory, like the carven ivories that were painted long ago in silver and gold and rich, dim enamels, and studded with burning gems.

'I mind,' said one, 'ah! I mind as if it was yesterday—'

At the magic of those words, 'I mind,' these pictures of the soul took shape and colour; from homely sentences and broken phrases, a sigh, a tear; so that to every eye in the room the dun-coloured walls were obliterated, glowing like painted windows, garlanded with memories, hung with the little eikons of forty-nine homes. Even the flat-faced materialist had possessed a home, and she was as jealous of its recollection as an ugly woman of a lover.

The balls of sad-coloured wool became inextricably tangled, as the exultant kitten seized her happy hour. Stockings were forgotten. Grey was forgotten. The matron was forgotten. Even the solemn festival that was to take place this very evening was forgotten.

'Cushat-doves!' murmured Fidelia in a low and dreamy voice. 'I kept cushat-doves. And my gyarden most always had a flower.'

'Dahlias was what our maister was set on,' said a very old woman with bright blue eyes. 'Ah! he liked a dahlia.'

'Roses, ours fancied,' put in the stout woman.

'Ah? I clem for the smell of a cabbage rose,' said Fidelia.

She became mysterious, and dived into the deep pocket of her skirt.

'Look ye! she whispered. 'I couldna bide all summer without the smell of a cabbage rose. And this morning they'd left the ladder by our ward windy, being fluskered with the Bishop coming. So I crep' out and went to the matron's gyarden afore it was light and pulled this 'ere.'

She held up a deep red rose amid cries of admiration and reproof.

And just as she held it up, the matron entered.

'That's the third time you've trespassed, broken bounds, and stolen,' said the matron wearily. She was a kind-hearted woman, but her promotion depended on the

104

strictness of her discipline. She was part of a machine. If it was a bad machine, she had neither time nor inclination to try to alter it.

'You'll stop away from service at the chapel to-night, and you won't go to the harvest tea at the Rectory,' said the matron. Fidelia's Egyptian profile was unmoved; but tears stood in her eyes. Festivals were very few, and the harvest tea was the event of the year.

There was a sound of wheels. The Bishop! He entered with the Rector and some ladies. Everyone stood up. Only the kitten remained umimpressed.

The Bishop had thought, as he saw the workhouse from a turn of the road, that it looked dreary. He had thought that it would be good to turn the eyes of these old women to the mansions of the blest. He was really kind and sympathetic, only he was not gifted with imagination, and he had never been an old, homesick, knitting woman on a bench.

So he said cheerfully, 'Suppose we sing

"Jerusalem, my happy home!"

and then, in lighter vein,

"Home, sweet home!"'

He intended to weave these into his speech, and only to bring in mention of the consecration of the chapel towards the end.

They sang,

'Jerusalem, my happy home!'

It was a little quavering, a little irregular, but that was put down to age.

Towards the end came an audible sound from Fidelia. Then they sang,

'Home, sweet home!'

What with the memories, and the talk, and Fidelia's sob, there were a good many sniffs and surreptitious wipings of eyes.

In the last line Fidelia flung her apron over her head and wept aloud.

'Thatcher!' said the matron.

'There, there!' soothed the Bishop; and he gave her shoulder a little pat, and told her to sit down, and was sure his speech would comfort her.

But, alas! his speech did not comfort. It lacerated. It destroyed the pictures that had glowed on the wall. It hammered to pieces the little eikons of home. It built up a picture of Heaven which had in it no touch of the loved fold and cottage, but which appeared to ninety-eight alarmed eyes to be exactly like the workhouse. It was grand and large and rather pompous. It had nothing in it of firelit evenings and the bit of sewing and father winding the clock. And the more the Bishop struggled to comfort a sorrow he could not grasp, the more formal he became.

When he had finished, Fidelia emerged from her apron, and her face was that of one who has been through an agony.

So that was Heaven!

No lilac. No pink rose, nor white rose. No work. No pink feet on the tiles. Nothing but an enormous, everlasting old women's ward built of solid gold, and without even a kitten.

She looked at the Bishop and beheld him as a thief, robbing her of all hope. She had thought, without exactly formulating her thought, that Heaven would be a place with homely corners in it where the poor might dwell as of old. This man was robbing her of her dream, and it was all she had. She stood up.

'It inna true!' she cried. 'It's words, words, words, a mort of words; but it inna true. And if it's true I dunna want it. It's for Squire and Rector and you. It inna for us. We'm lost our whomes; we'm gone back to school like, after working 'ard a many years. And if the Lord, as was but a carpenter's prentice 'isself, and the Lord's Mother, as was but a carpenter's wife, canna give poor folk a bit o' comfort in the next world, I dunna want to go there.'

She sat down and retired into her apron. Every face in the lines of benches was strained forward towards the group that symbolized authority, waiting for doom to fall.

'Matron,' said the Bishop, 'the poor thing's overwrought.'

'Not quite herself,' said the Rector's wife.

'A little—queer. A little—wandering,' added another lady.

'Do not punish her,' said the Bishop. 'The day must not be darkened.'

'But she's hardly responsible, is she?' said a guardian.

The matron, trembling with distress and wrath, whispered to the Rector:

'The asylum side?'

'Yes, yes,' said the Rector in what he meant to be a whisper, 'the asylum side.' But he was a hearty man, used to open-air sports, and his whisper was quite audible.

The visitors went away to tea at the Rectory. Service was not till seven. The old women filed out to their mugs of tea and slabs of bread and margarine. Fidelia remained where she was—a derelict. Discipline was momentarily relaxed because she did not count any more. The asylum side! The asylum side! She could not understand it. She, Fidelia Thatcher, the best butter-maker in the district, a self-respecting, self-supporting woman, had come to this. To-morrow she would be like a dumb beast driven hither and thither, under physical authority, bathed by attendants, slapped, taken for walks in a drove with imbeciles and lunatics—mad. No home on earth. No home in Heaven—if the Bishop was right.

'No!' she muttered. 'It's lies, what he says.' To-morrow, blackness of darkness; but she had to-night. She must think. She must efface herself to gain time.

The old women's room had a door opening into a paved, flowerless space which ought to have been a garden. Under the roof of the porch was a swallow's nest, hydra-headed with young. Fidelia loved to see the parent birds dart to and fro. She had watched them since they brought the first dabs of mud, until now when the young were ready to fly. She brought out a bench. No one ever came here in the evenings. They would go to the service and forget her. With folded hands, she sat in her corner so still that the birds were not afraid of her.

'Wings!' she murmured. 'Wings!'

But there were no wings for her. Even if she desired to creep away and die by the roadside, she could not, for across the workhouse entrance was a locked gate. She watched the swallows flash across the slack clothes-line on which the grey stockings were dried, dart to the nest with that infinitesimal pause in which the food is miraculously transferred from beak to beak, and sweep away into the silent evening. And the swallows put into her mind what she would do. She fetched the yard broom, and raked down the nest.

'Fly!' she said. 'Ye can!'

The four young swallows were gone into the soft, dove-coloured evening. From the chapel came the sound of the anthem.

'Blessed are the meek.'

Fidelia, with the broom in her hand, looked at the broken house of clay.

'It inna true,' she said to the depths of grey air. 'They binna blessed. Them as is blessed is them as can fly.'

With steady fingers she untied the clothes-line, and looped it over the beam of the porch. She drew forth her rose and smelt it. She saw again the pink rose-tree and the white rose-tree and the lilac. She climbed on to the bench.

'This minute,' she said to herself, 'I be a pauper lunatic by the mercy of men. The next minute I'll make a trial of the mercy of God. Fidelia Thatcher, fly! Ye can!'

And just as the concluding strains of 'Blessed are the meek' sounded harmoniously, Fidelia Thatcher stepped off the bench.